Colusa County Free Library

738 Market Street
Colusa, CA   95932
Phone : 458-7671

By George Bagby

TWO IN THE BUSH

KILLER BOY WAS HERE

HONEST RELIABLE CORPSE

ANOTHER DAY—ANOTHER
DEATH

CORPSE CANDLE

DIRTY POOL

MYSTERIOUSER AND
MYSTERIOUSER

MURDER'S LITTLE HELPER

EVIL GENIUS

THE REAL GONE GOOSE

THE THREE-TIME LOSERS

DEAD WRONG

COP KILLER

DEAD STORAGE

A DIRTY WAY TO DIE

THE BODY IN THE BASKET

DEAD DRUNK

GIVE THE LITTLE CORPSE A
BIG HAND

THE CORPSE WITH STICKY
FINGERS

SCARED TO DEATH

DEATH AIN'T COMMERCIAL

BLOOD WILL TELL

COFFIN CORNER

DROP DEAD

IN COLD BLOOD

THE STARTING GUN

THE TWIN KILLING

THE ORIGINAL CARCASE

DEAD ON ARRIVAL

MURDER CALLING "50"

RED IS FOR KILLING

HERE COMES THE CORPSE

THE CORPSE WORE A WIG

THE CORPSE WITH THE
PURPLE THIGHS

BIRD WALKING WEATHER

MURDER ON THE NOSE

MURDER HALF-BAKED

RING AROUND A MURDER

MURDER AT THE PIANO

BACHELORS' WIFE

TWO IN THE BUSH

TWO IN THE BUSH

GEORGE BAGBY

PUBLISHED FOR THE CRIME CLUB BY

DOUBLEDAY & COMPANY, INC.

GARDEN CITY, NEW YORK

1976

All of the characters in this book
are fictitious, and any resemblance
to actual persons, living or dead,
is purely coincidental.

9089677

Library of Congress Cataloging in Publication Data

Stein, Aaron Marc, 1906–
Two in the bush.

I. Title.
PZ3.S819Ty [PS3569.T34]   813'.5'2
ISBN 0-385-11438-9
Library of Congress Catalog Card Number 75–21208

First Edition

For
Margaret and Philip
Manhard
in admiration of
their courage
and
with the author's
love

TWO IN THE BUSH

I am a New Yorker, one of the natives. I was born on Manhattan Island and between its two rivers I grew up. I have lived here ever since. Even when I've been long away from New York, I've always kept a Manhattan place to come back to and I suppose I always shall.

In the light of which you could be expecting that I will be the typical New Yorker. I am not. What's become of the other people who were born on Manhattan Island and who back when we were kids played with me in Central Park I don't know. That's the nature of the place. You lose people in its size and its ferment. More than that, I suspect that there aren't too many of us who stick it out without making off to the suburbs and beyond. Among my friends today I can name only one who, like myself, is a native Manhattanite and who all his life has called the island home.

That's Inspector Schmidt, chief of Homicide, NYPD. We never knew each other as kids, never played together or any of that. We were both well along and established in our respective professions before we first met. Schmitty had already risen through the departmental ranks to his present eminence and I had already published before either of us dreamed of what has now been this long association in which I make books out of the inspector's investigations.

But I was saying that I am not a typical New Yorker. Nor is Inspector Schmidt. Your typical New Yorker is a refugee from some place like Iowa or Indiana and he is so bent on living down his beginnings that he makes a full-time job of being the big-city boy, not even faintly tainted with any such cornball characteristics as neighborliness. He is without human curiosity and without human sympathy. People are murdered on his doorstep and he dismisses their cries of pain and their appeals for help as just some more city sounds. In the country you might have birdsong. In the city it's death rattles.

Those are your typical New Yorkers and they couldn't be more different from me. I'm just a plain, old-fashioned, home-town boy. I'm neighborly. I know the people who live around me. I have a gossipy, back-fence curiosity about them, and that's not all. I care about them.

Anytime I go out of my own little corner of Manhattan I do have the metropolitan experience, but except for those times when Inspector Schmidt has a particularly interesting case going and he has me following him around on it, my forays out of the home neighborhood are not too frequent. I can go for days without venturing beyond walking range of the home pad and for weeks without hitting a day of which the far greater part has not been spent around the home district.

The block I live in is a contributing factor, though I don't think it's done anything toward making me the way I am. It is far more likely that it is because of the way I am that I have chosen to live in such an area. I have an apartment, but it doesn't sit in the upper reaches of one of the great towers. On our block we scrape no skies. We are townhouses or, as is the case of the one I live in, one-time townhouses that have been broken up into apartments. We are uniformly five stories tall and we turn our backs on the city. We have taken down all the fences that stood between our various back yards and we've pooled the collected space into one cooperatively maintained garden. Each of us pays his share of the gardener's wage and the other upkeep costs and we all of us have joint use and enjoyment of the garden. We've shaped our houses to it and we shape our lives to it. In as much of our living as we can manage we include the view of our garden. We have shoved our kitchens and bathrooms and such off to the street side of our houses and apartments. Our bedrooms and living rooms, our studies and dining rooms are rooms with a view, the view of our garden. So, however much with shades or blinds or screens we hide ourselves away from the stranger who passes along our street, on our garden side we keep ourselves wide open. This, of course, is the city aspect of it. If we would look out on our garden, we must accept that we are looked in on by our garden neighbors.

I've been told that there are cities in the American heartland where everyone lives that much and even more in the public view, communities where a drawn shade is taken to be prima facie evidence that something shameful is being done behind it. Ours, however, is not a society which recognizes no privacy other than concealment. We accept the fact that, if we are all to have uninterrupted garden viewing, we must make one of those big-city bargains for the pleasure. We trade off against it all genuine privacy.

Are you asking what other kind there is? There's the kind which by a civilized pretense we fall back upon. It is a fiction of privacy sustained by a self-deception that by tacit agreement we all of us practice. We know that we are seeing and being seen but we pretend that we do not and are not. We manage this pretense in all ordinary times. All the people who live across the garden from me and any of the others who sit out in the garden or stroll its paths know that Inspector Schmidt never drops in on me but that he immediately shucks out of his shoes and pads around my place in his socks. Nobody has so much as mentioned it. Nobody has shown the first bit of curiosity about the inspector's feet.

It's not that in New York he isn't a celebrity. He is. It isn't that he goes unrecognized by my neighbors or that they are not interested in him or curious about him. They are. Given an opportunity, they will ask all manner of questions about him; but, under that civilized understanding by which we operate, seeing him through my garden windows is not an opportunity. A neighbor might open up a conversation about the inspector by remarking that he'd seen Schmitty come up the street on his way to see me or that he'd noticed the inspector's official car parked out in front of the house. Out in the street we are visible. Through our garden windows we are by agreement invisible.

For myself I must confess that I do enjoy my grandstand seat for observing my neighbors as much perhaps as I enjoy the garden. I did suspect all along that I was not alone in this, that my neighbors were having the same sort of fun. When violence came to live with us in this quiet and peaceful corner of ours and brought death with it, our pretense perforce broke down and for the first time we were speaking of what each of us saw through the other man's windows and nobody could be surprised that others had been looking quite as much as he had himself.

The first break in our fabric of protective fiction came from the most unexpected quarter. Daphne Hobbes spoke out and ripped it open. Daphne Hobbes was English. Daphne Hobbes was rich. At a glance anyone could see that she was by many years our oldest resident and, even if we hadn't had our grandstand seats for observing the way Daphne Hobbes lived, it would have been obvious to all of us that hers was a way of life unlike the way the rest of us lived.

The house she had across the garden from me was only one of the domiciles she maintained. Although it wasn't until later that I learned the particulars—that there was a London flat in Eaton Square, a country house in Somerset, and a place in the sun on an island in the Bahamas—I did know that she occupied her New York house only through part of the year. Some years it would be the spring, others the autumn. The inclement seasons—the heat of the summer and the cold and wet of winter—she was never with us, but her house didn't stand empty while she was away. A young man occupied it then. It was reported around the block that he was a relative, something like a grandnephew. When she was in residence, he dined with her once a week. Sometimes it would be a small dinner party, other weeks even smaller, just the two of them alone. Either way it was always black tie and menus that ran to lobster and pheasant and such and never less than three wine glasses at each place.

When she would be away and he appeared across the garden as a resident and not as a dinner guest, it would be jeans and a sweatshirt in winter, shorts and skin in summer, and his meals, taken alone, ran to simpler fare and to beer swigged from the can.

It was early May and Daphne Hobbes had been in residence only a matter of weeks after having been away all winter. She was looking well. I would have guessed that she'd had a good winter, but for all her appearance of ruddy good health, I did wonder this one morning whether some form of senile dementia might not have set in. She was doing something I had never seen her do before. She seemed to be on a telephoning jag. She had settled herself at the phone in her bedroom with a tea tray and a sheet of paper. She dialed one call after another and drank one cup of tea after another. When the teapot would turn up empty, she would leave the phone but only for long enough to replenish the tea. Then she would come straight back to the phone and pick up where she'd left off, telephoning and tea drinking.

There was nothing unusual about all the tea. I had noticed that about her all along. Anytime she was not at table or asleep and she didn't have a teacup in her hand, you would be certain that she wasn't far from one. The telephoning was odd. She was making so many calls and they might all have been the same call. I didn't hold a watch on them, but they were all of about the same length and her lips seemed to go through exactly the same movements for each. She could have been calling every last person she knew and delivering to each the same short, prepared speech.

Describing it this way does make it seem peculiar enough, but I don't know that just on the tea and the telephoning I would have been moved to watch her so closely that I would have noticed the strange uniformity of all the calls. There was this other thing she did and that was so peculiar and looked so mad that it did set me to watching her and noticing the rest of it.

During a good half of these calls she was making she also seemed to be carrying on some sort of flirtation with people in the houses on my side of the garden. She would look fixedly at one set of windows or another in houses alongside the one my apartment is in. She would smile and nod and twinkle and wave until the moment she hung up on that call. Then for another call she would go through an identical set of gestures and grimaces but now directed at another bank of windows.

She had me in such a fever of curiosity with this performance that I quite forgot that one of the ways we had of preserving our protective fiction was the great skill we'd all developed in the trick of watching without seeming to watch. I was just standing at my window and gaping at her.

Making another check mark on her paper—it was evidently a list and she was checking off a name as she completed each call—she turned to look at my windows. Our eyes met briefly but she quickly turned away to dial another number. In hot confusion I left my window wondering whether she mightn't be aware of the spectacle she'd been making of herself and expecting that she would be bitterly resentful of me for having watched her do it.

When my phone rang, it slipped my mind that I had seen her consult her list before she'd dialed her next number. I was certain that it would be she on the telephone and that she was about to tell me what she thought of my manners. But then I picked up the phone and it was she and I did recall that she had dialed my number just as she had all the others, glancing at her paper before putting her finger in to dial. This call to me, then, was to be just another in the series and not occasioned by her having caught me looking.

I carried my phone to the window.

"Mr. Bagby," she said. "Daphne Hobbes here."

Seeing me back at the window, she broke out in the big smile. She nodded. She waved.

I mumbled something, still not certain that I wasn't to swing into explanation and apology. She talked right on over my mumble.

"Would you do me the great favor, Mr. Bagby, of coming across the garden at six o'clock today to take a glass of wine with me? I must speak with you about something which concerns all of us. I am asking all of the residents. What I have to tell you is important. It is shocking, but it is not complicated. I can promise you that you won't be kept long."

I found my voice and told her I would be free at six and would be happy to come across the garden. She thanked me and I thanked her and she brought reinforcement up behind her every word by pantomiming her pleasure. Automatically I responded, matching her grin for grin and wave for wave. I had to show a pleasure that might be some sort of a match to hers.

At one minute before six I stepped out into the garden. Up and down the rows of houses that closed it around, doors were opening even as I had opened mine. She had asked all of us and every last one of us was coming. The unanimity was impressive and I was certain that the others were being driven by just those same forces as were driving me, curiosity about the important and shocking news our hostess had promised us but, even more than that perhaps, curiosity about our hostess herself.

I've already told you she was English, rich, and advanced in years. She had that weather-beaten look I have always thought to be peculiarly British. It is the look of good stuff that has been long used and has worn well—old leather, ancient tweed. She had the high-bridged, narrow nose that should have given her a beaky look, but she carried it too high for that. She looked as though she were always sniffing out the world around her and scenting nothing she didn't disdain. If she was indeed perpetually making adverse judgments, however, there was nothing but the angle of her nose to indicate it. Her mouth was gentle and her eyes were kind.

As we entered from the garden it wasn't at all certain that what had sounded like a summons to a business meeting was not in actuality an invitation to a cocktail party, but one of staggering formality. Our hostess' maid—she had one who came in by the day and I knew her from seeing her across the garden—was on hand, but she had been supplemented with a bartender and a formidable butler type who, stationed just inside the french doors that gave access from the garden, asked each of us his name so that he could feed it back to us in stentorian announcement.

The maid was passing champagne and advising all and sundry that if anyone wanted something else, he need only make his way to the bar and take up his needs with the bartender. Mrs. Hobbes waited till there was nobody without drink before she took her stance in front of the bar and launched into her formal address. She seemed every inch the duchess come to open the bazaar.

"Dear friends," she said. "I cannot begin but by thanking you for coming to me this evening. You are busy people. Your time is valuable and I fully appreciate the generosity of your giving it for what must seem to you to be nothing more than the self-indulgent whim of an idle old bag."

Later, as I came to know her better, I did grow accustomed to the way she talked. That, however, doesn't mean she ever lost her capacity for astonishing me. She had that accent which to a British ear would mean everything and which, just by the shaping of its vowels, would tell where she was born, how she was educated, and at precisely which rung of the social ladder she was located. On one occasion she commented on it herself.

"It's the sound one makes," she said, "when one has learned to talk around the silver spoon in one's mouth. If one has been born with the bloody thing, how can one expect to talk like people who have unencumbered tongues?"

What she didn't say and what in any conversation one had with her soon became obvious was that she was so secure in this accent she pretended to deplore that she felt free to allow herself to say anything she pleased. Profanities, obscenities, vulgarisms, and even Americanisms were all permissible on her lips since they were so impeccably uttered that no one could ever make the mistake of thinking that she was using them by anything but deliberate choice. A slovenly speaker of less aristocractic intonations might use words like "bag" and "bloody" because he knew no better. She used them in full knowledge of what she was doing and in full confidence that she stood above criticism.

Since for most, if not all, of us, however, this was the first time, her "old bag" elicited from the crowd an astonished gasp or two and a general murmur of demurral.

She swept on past it. "If I move straight to the point, therefore," she said, "and dispose of our problems with all possible speed, it is not, you must believe me, because I am in haste to have you out of here. It is only so that those of you who do have other engagements won't be delayed while I stumble through preambles designed to break the news to you gently. The fact, I am sorry to tell you, is ugly. Nothing anyone can say will avail to make it less ugly. Since anything that occurs in our garden must, I am certain, concern all of us, I have not felt like acting alone. It is our joint concern. We should act jointly and that is only if there should be any necessity for acting at all. Obviously all of us would be relieved to have it that we need not take any action. Unfortunately, however, we can have that relief only in the event that the culprit should be one of us, and we certainly shall not wish for that."

For someone who was going to drive straight to the point and not delay us with any preambles, she seemed to be finding a great many words along the way, but I couldn't see that anyone was minding her verbosity. The champagne was dry. What little could be made of what she was saying seemed intriguing. There had been an ugly occurrence in our garden and she was expecting us to take some sort of joint action because of it unless it would develop that the culprit was one of us. I couldn't see how that would free us of the need for action and I looked about me in the expectation, I suppose, of surprising a guilty look on the face of one of the neighbors. I surprised nothing. My looks only met theirs. All of us, in equal conviction of our own innocence, were looking about for what Mrs. Hobbes was calling the culprit.

She paused for a moment. She might have been waiting for one of us to step up to the bar and make a confession of sin. Nobody moved.

"I have the evidence to show," she said. "I have it here. I expect it will speak for itself."

Whipping around the end of her bar, she stepped behind it and bent down. For only a moment or two she was gone out of sight. When she bobbed up again it was with a paper plate in her hand. On the plate lay a dead bird. It was a large bird and it had been dead for some time. Displaying the thing which she'd just said would speak for itself, she spoke for it.

Explaining that it was a dead hawk, she went into considerable ornithological detail about what she called "this splendid bird." No need to quote her in full. The main points of her disquisition will suffice, and they were that this had been no ordinary hawk but a variety much admired by bird-fanciers. Bird-fanciers, furthermore, were doing a lot of worrying about these much-admired hawks because there seemed to be a good possibility that they wouldn't be having any of them to admire for very long. They were one of the threatened species and even with the most assiduous application of protective measures there was no certainty that these birds could survive. Even now there might not be enough of them left to breed themselves back from where they were standing at the brink of extinction. With much luck and the maximum of protection they just might do it. If people shot them there would be no hope.

"I am not opposed to shooting," the lady said. "At the right time, in the right place, knowledgeable guns out after a suitable quarry—it's excellent sport. The city, I submit, is not the right place. The time? We are not in the small-game season. Actually at the moment we are in the season for the shooting of any game, so we cannot say that some bad shot, legitimately but clumsily and unskillfully after a permitted quarry, hit the hawk by mistake, because these birds are protected. There is never an open season on them."

Brandishing the anything-but-splendid remains of her "splendid bird" before us, she conceded that she had no knowledge of how the rest of us might stand on such things as conservation or gun control. She had brought us together

to deal with this matter because she did feel confident that
we were all at one in our interest in our garden.

"I found it there this morning," she said. "It was in most
distressing condition. Cats had been at it, but no cat had
killed it. Cats do not fill a bird with shot, but even before I
had examined it, I knew it hadn't fallen victim to a cat. In
the unlikely circumstance of a struggle between one of these
birds and even the fiercest of cats, the bird would inevitably
and always come off the winner. On examination the cause
of death became obvious. The poor thing had been shot
down, wantonly slaughtered by a gun in our garden. You can
see for yourself."

With those words she thrust it at Flora Gibbons and I
don't think there was anyone in that room who thought she
had chosen to begin with Mrs. Gibbons by accident or
through any misapplication of a notion of "ladies first."
There could hardly be any one of us who might be ignorant
of the identity of our local gun. It would have to be Eric
Gibbons, the lady's teenage son. There had been complaints
about Eric from time to time, but previously it had always
been air-rifle pellets shot at windows across the garden.

They had never been my windows, but I couldn't delude
myself that it was because the boy liked me better than he
did any of the other neighbors. My immunity could be at-
tributed to the geography of our apartments. The Gibbons
family was among my nearest neighbors. They had an apartment in the house next door to me, a large, family-size
triplex in contrast to my ground-floor, single-occupancy job.
They were a family of three, a couple with the one son, and
on those occasions when young Eric had taken target practice on the windows readily available, it had, of course, been
the windows across the garden that had suffered.

Whether the summons to drink and discussion had been
intended to include Eric Gibbons or not I didn't know. I
could easily imagine that it had only been by his father's de-

cision that he was not in attendance. I know that if I were the father of so hulkingly large and unremittingly loutish a fifteen-year-old, I would be trying to postpone as long as possible the pup's introduction to alcohol.

They had always seemed a dull family. Bill Gibbons, the father, officially known as William C., had from the first struck me as the most improbable progenitor that boy could have had. At the time of these events we had been neighbors for about two years and I don't think I can remember a time when the kid didn't outweigh his father. The elder Gibbons was short and slight. Small-boned and spare of frame, he always seemed fit enough but never sufficiently muscular even to be called wiry. The kid, on the other hand, appeared to be everything his father was not. The big, pudgy youngster had, at about age thirteen, shot past his father's sum of inches and at about the same time had begun the hardening of his pudginess that had been converting him into a thick-necked hunk of mindless muscle. I never saw the boy without being reminded of beef cattle in a feed lot. He had the characteristic look of the animal raised for meat, a fifty-fifty mix of power and torpor.

The boy's mother, though bigger than her husband, was no Amazon, in no respect the sort of woman you would figure for producing giants. She was a moderately pretty woman and immoderately silly. She was given to simpering and fluttering and giggling. She was also given to baby talk and, if she had any purpose in life, it would have to be an ambition to be the first woman over thirty to take up from high-school girls each of their fashion fads in turn. I can remember bobby socks and, as the one-time wearers of bobby socks had been growing up, Flora Gibbons had been maintaining her steady course of growing down, passing successively through pedalpushers, miniskirts, maxicoats, granny glasses, gypsy patches, and hotpants.

If you want to get the picture, you must combine this assiduous pursuit of childish disguises with the way she treated her husband. You had to assume that at some point she had been a wife to the man, since they had produced Eric, but you'd never catch her acting the part. Her role was always that of the loving daughter and it wasn't only that in referring to him she was wont to call him daddy. It was the whole filial bit.

If you are reading all this to mean she was anybody's child bride, forget it. Her husband was no more an old man than she was the baby doll she imagined herself to be. I would say that the two of them were pretty much of an age, give or take the year or two that could easily have gone either way. He wasn't even one of those settled types who seems old beyond his years. His movements were quick and precise and his manner brisk and incisive. He was every inch the business executive just come into early middle age but already well established in a solid success and still full of push and upward mobility.

He was away a good deal of the time. Business trips were frequent and on many of these trips he took his lady with him, and then Eric would be left alone except for the couple they had working for them. When the boy was younger and papa and mama would both be away, the couple would sleep in so the kid wasn't alone in the apartment at night. For at least a year prior to the wine-and-hawk wingding the boy had evidently been thought old enough and responsible enough to be left on his own. The couple had been coming in as always during the day, but Eric had been fending for himself by night.

If prior to that afternoon you had asked me what family relations were like in the Gibbons household, I think I could have told you something about the mother-son relationship. That had always been in line with the lady's babyish pretenses. In the earlier years, it had seemed to me, she treated the kid as though he were only her brattish younger brother, a nuisance and a pain, and if on occasion she showed a flash of affection for the boy, there was always something in her manner to let you know that the sentiment was a manifestation of a good little girl's sweetness and generosity.

Once her son's voice changed, however, and the first signs of down began sprouting on his chin and lip, all that went through a quick metamorphosis. She began treating him as an equal except that this was a lady without the first breath of Women's Lib ideas. He was the big, strong man and she was the poor, weak, defenseless woman and she never missed a chance to let the young lug know it. So I suppose it was hardly Eric's fault that there was never a fifteen-year-old more urgently in need of slapping down.

On what I've been telling you about them, you must be assuming that the kid's father would just not be man enough to handle him. The physical disparity, of course, was obvious. Eric could have flattened his old man with no more than a flip of one of his meaty hands, but somehow you never thought about them in those terms. Bill Gibbons always appeared to be in command. It was the crisp efficiency of his manner. He brought home with him from the business world all the authority of the major executive. He was the man who gave the orders and he was the man who would have unquestioning obedience. That he approached the domestic scene with an air of abstraction, as though his mind were elsewhere engaged with weightier matters than wives and children, might have meant that this obedience was so much an automatic thing in his home that there was no need for him to give his wife or son anything more than this offhand fraction of his attention. It was also possible that, through this very inattention to matters domestic, he was deluding himself about the power he wielded in the family circle. He could be assuming that he had the obedience even though it had never been put to the test. You needn't worry about how your orders will be taken if you never give any orders.

So Mrs. Hobbes shoved her paper plate with the hawk on it at Mrs. Gibbons. Baby doll backed away from it, but Mrs. Hobbes was relentless.

"It was in anything but agreeable condition when I picked it up in the garden," she said, "but I popped it straight into the bar fridge—the ice-making thing, you know —and it's thoroughly frozen. It will be only as it thaws that it will begin to stink again. It's quite inoffensive now."

If these assurances had been intended to make Flora Gibbons more receptive to the frozen cadaver of the hawk, they were a spectacular failure. The lady's retreat from the paper plate that was being urged upon her speeded up to a backward run. She had almost backed all the way to the broad glass doors that stood open to the garden when she thought to take her transfixed gaze from the plate and transfer it to the glass of champagne she was still holding in her hand.

"The bar fridge," she gulped. "You've had that thing . . ."

She couldn't finish. Completely overcome, she let the glass fall from her fingers. It shattered and wine formed a little bubbling pool on Mrs. Hobbes' floor. Turning on her heel, Mrs. Gibbons fled into the garden. A flicker of amusement passed over our hostess' lips. A smile that could have been more firmly curbed?

"So sorry," she said in a tone that was anything but sorry. "I'm always doing that. I just can't keep my mind on vegetarians, and I was so pleased with myself for thinking of the bar fridge. After all, I never put ice into anything, and the silly thing goes on and on making the cubes. At long last it was good for something. I *was* pleased."

She looked around at her other guests. Nobody was reacting as spectacularly as had Mrs. Gibbons, but no few people quietly set their wine glasses aside and concentrated on a greening of their faces which was never what Charles Reich meant. Not all of the greening faces, furthermore, belonged to the ladies among us.

"Let's not all be silly," Mrs. Hobbes resumed. "The wine was solidly corked all the time it was being iced. The bottles weren't opened until after they had come out of the fridge."

None of the discarded wine glasses was picked up again. Another one, in fact, was firmly rejected. Bill Gibbons, while with his free hand he took from her the paper plate with the hawk on it, simultaneously pushed into her grasp his glass of champagne.

"You've made your point, Mrs. Hobbes," he said. "You've made all your points. You need go no further. I'll dispose of this thing and you have my guarantee that there will be no more shooting in the garden. Send me your bill for the wine glass Mrs. Gibbons lacked the strength to hold."

"The glass doesn't matter, Mr. Gibbons."

She was about to tell him what did matter, but he wasn't hanging around to hear any more.

"But it does matter, Mrs. Hobbes," he said. "I've been cured of an expensive taste. I'll be saving the cost of the glass many times over, since I won't be drinking champagne after this."

Taking the dead hawk with him, he marched out to the garden. Mrs. Hobbes, at her garden door, watched him till he had gone all the way across and on into his own place. Returning to the rest of us, she was smiling.

"I like the man," she said. "Even though he is that weak in the tum—so weak that the poor bird put him off his wine—he hasn't allowed it to interfere with doing what he must. It is precisely what I should have done if the lad were a son of mine. He shot the hawk. Disposing of it is the least part of what ought now be required of that young man."

Her maid and the barman had already dealt with the spilled champagne and the shards of shattered glass. Confronted with the array of less spectacularly rejected glasses of wine and with a green face she could match up to each of those glasses, she exerted herself to make amends. Allowing that it might even have been naughty of her to permit so unpleasant a misunderstanding to persist once it had arisen, she excused herself on the ground that she couldn't abide silly women and in her experience she had never known one sillier than Flora Gibbons.

Although she had frozen the dead hawk in her bar icemaker, it was exactly as she had said. That was the only use she had ever found for what she considered the most superfluous of gadgets.

"The ice for chilling the wine came out of the kitchen," she said. "That absurd thing in the bar will probably never be used for anything again. I hardly anticipate another occasion on which I shall want to preserve something dead in the place where it would be most at hand for me when I might want to place it on display in my drawing room."

In a few of the faces the color improved. Of these few, furthermore, some even recovered enough to go back to sipping the excellent champagne. We hardy souls who had never relinquished our glasses—and there were no few of us—just went on as before. The stricken and unrecovered made their excuses and hurried away. Mrs. Hobbes made no effort to keep them. Having seen the last of them out to the garden, she didn't even wait for them to be out of earshot. You must know that she had the clear, perfectly projected voice and the precision of enunciation that made earshot in her case a dimension of no mean distance.

"Now that," she said, "separated the men from the boys, and we've a great quantity of wine to drink up. So you must help me. I don't like getting sloshed alone. Nobody else may leave until the last drop's been drunk. Sloshed is right, isn't it? I do love Americanisms but I sometimes have the feeling that I don't always get them straight."

So we settled in to lap up all the champagne that had

been opened. A few of the couples were staying on and all the men who had come alone but most notably Jill Armitage hung on till the last drop had been wrung out of the last bottle. Jill was our divorcee. Over the years she had been our divorcee again and again, more times than anyone bothers to count. She owned the house next door to where I live, the one where the Gibbons family were her tenants in the triplex. Above them is a duplex which served Jill as her vacation home. Each time she went on vacation from one of her marriages she returned to it. Each time she took a fresh set of vows she left it for whatever premises the sucker she married might have provided, and for the duration of that bout of conjugal bliss she put a tenant in her duplex. Come the time that she left that husband's bed and board, she got the tenant out and again took up residence herself. One school of thought around the garden held that the duration of each of her marriages was contingent on the length of the duplex tenant's lease. Another argued that her marriages curdled at their own pace and that the lady had a special talent for breaking a tenant's lease. I don't know.

The way I began telling you about our Jill, I may have suggested to you that it would have been the champagne that held her. I must set that right. Drink was not Jill Armitage's thing. Men were. She could take drink or leave it alone, although I cannot remember ever having seen her leave it alone. Men? Assemble yourself a roomful of unattached males anywhere or even of semidetached ones and let Jill Armitage get wind of it. That was all, brother.

She stayed and she worked hard at being the life of Daphne Hobbes' party.

In no time at all they were "Daff, baby" and "my most dear Gillian."

II

There are times when Inspector Schmidt has an investigation going and it is into a murder more lurid than most.
It's a big story for the papers and later, when I shall be
doing the full account of it, it will be a big story for me. At
such times I make a point of seeing all the rags.

The morning after Daphne Hobbes wined all her neighbors, however, wasn't one of those days. I had the *Times*
with my coffee and I didn't bother with any other paper.
You know the New York *Times*. It's a lot of paper even if
you're no more than skimming it. So although I was taking
my breakfast at one of my garden windows, I was looking at
nothing but coffee, toast, and newsprint.

The *Times* and I were clear around the other side of the
world, somewhere East probably Far or Near, when the
ringing of my phone brought me back to the actualities of
my surroundings. I dropped the paper and reached for the
phone. The paper downed, I was, of course, looking out at
the garden and across it to the Hobbes' windows. Daphne
was at it again, equally engaged with telephone and teacup,
but dimpling and twinkling and bobbing at me. Catching
my eye, she set aside the cup so she could pick up a folded
newspaper and wave it at me. I'd been through something
too like this the day before. I wasn't in the least surprised
that it was the lady calling me.

"Daphne Hobbes here," she said. "George, you are a pet.
I've just read it and it's most delicious. I cannot believe
some newspaper person wrote it from what you told him.

It's much too witty for that. You wrote it for him, didn't you?"

At the start of that I was vain enough to think she had picked up one of my books and was calling to tell me how much she'd enjoyed it, but not even vanity could squeeze the whole of what she was saying into any such shape.

"What's delicious?" I asked.

"Your newspaper article about the hawk and the bar fridge and the gorgeously rising gorge of the Gibbons pair. I almost said the pair of Gibbons. They did make monkeys of themselves, didn't they?"

Delighted with her pun, she tinkled a happy laugh into the phone.

"What newspaper article?"

Across the garden she flipped a hand at me. You know that oh-go-along-with-you gesture.

"Of course, I shan't say a word about it to anyone but you," she promised. "We haven't the faintest notion of how any of it got into the paper. I'm no fool. I know that we have to go on living with them and it's been much too pleasant for all of us to let hard feelings come in and spoil it. Especially for you, right next door to them as you are. It wouldn't matter as much to me. I can sit over here and make faces at them if it should come to that, but where you are, it could be awkward for you. I can readily understand why you didn't sign it, and I'm no fool, George. Not to worry. I shan't betray you."

I disowned her newspaper article. I didn't leave it with simply denying that I had written it or had even furnished a reporter with the material for writing it. I explained that, although my book-length reports on Inspector Schmidt's investigations could be considered a form of journalism, I had no connection with any daily paper.

"As a matter of fact," I said, "my attitude toward the dailies and even toward the weekly and monthly news rags is a bit on the hostile side. Anything they publish about material I am working on is that superficial quickie which takes the edge off an event without doing any proper exploration of it. It's always a worry. Will the papers have killed me off before I can hope to publish?"

I did think that was clear and explicit enough, but she knew better. There was nothing I could say that she didn't contrive to read in her own way. Her little evening had been written up. Since writing was done by writers and since I was a writer and I had been the only writer present, QED. I had rushed into print and had given no one the time to be there before me and take the edge off what I had to say. I had been nimble as well as clever. She was congratulating me on both counts.

I did try to convince her. At the risk of hurting her feelings, I explained what a nothing event her little evening had been. Nothing had happened, nothing that anyone in his right mind could have considered news.

With a wink so broad that it carried clear across the garden, she said the words that without the wink would have meant I'd made my point and that she was going along with me. The wink said quite the opposite. She would say whatever I wanted her to say. If I wanted it to be our secret, it was okay with her, but she and I knew better and wasn't it all the most delicious fun?

Naturally I couldn't let it go without seeing the deliciously witty prose she was so certain could have come from no typewriter but Bagby's. I left my *Times* and nipped down to the corner newsstand, where I picked up a copy of the rag she'd been flapping at me.

It was there, all of it, and I cannot say any of the quotes was inaccurate or even presented unfairly out of context.

It took the form of a society-page piece, a deadpan account of the newest development in the art of party giving as practiced in jet-set circles. It was careful of its use of names. Only the hostess and one of her guests were specifically identified. The rest of us remained nameless, though for anyone with more than the most casual familiarity with our corner of the town, many of us were sufficiently described to be readily identifiable.

Although the Gibbons family did share in the general anonymity, they figured most prominently in the story and were handled with so outrageous a lack of charity that, by comparison, it could seem as though Daphne Hobbes, in her treatment of that unfortunate pair, had been kind. It was no problem guessing which of the neighbors it was who had furnished the writer with his material. The news source had to be Jill Armitage. The prose of the piece reflected all too much of her characteristically acid tone, but even more revealing was the fact that, apart from our hostess, Jill was the only person mentioned in that newspaper account who was identified by name. The damn thing came close to being a publicity blast for la Armitage.

I didn't like it. If, through her misunderstanding, it had moved Daphne Hobbes to take me on as her special buddy, it seemed to me that this would be only a small part of what could be expected to result from the publication of that newspaper account. If the other neighbors were to jump to the same erroneous conclusion and tag me as the author of the nasty little piece, I could see myself becoming our garden group's Public Enemy No. 1. Mockery isn't likely to endear you to the mocked, and it wasn't only the Gibbons pair who had caught the barbs. I'd always had friendly relations with many of the nauseated and, although none of them had been identified by name, there were all those descriptive bits that made them far too recognizable.

Carrying the scurrilous rag with me, I nipped next door to have it out with Jill. Not finding her home, I promised myself that I would try again. I couldn't just leave it for my

neighbors to think what they would. On my way back I had
the ill luck to run into Lolly Gibbons in the garden. If you're
thinking Lolly might be a shortening of Lolita, forget it.

Her given name was Flora, but around our garden she
was mostly known as Lolly. Only rarely did any of us have
the stomach for calling her by all of the name her husband
used. That was Lollypop, which was fair enough. You must
know that, although she never referred to him except as
Daddy, she always addressed him as Tootsie Roll. I'm not
kidding. They were that kind of a couple.

She spotted the newspaper I was carrying folded under
my arm. She couldn't help noticing that I had it folded to
our story. She pouted. She waggled a finger at me. She
shifted her focus from me to the paper and she stuck her
tongue out at it.

"That column," I said, "nobody you would ever want to
know reads it. In fact, that goes for the whole dirty rag.
Who reads the filthy thing?"

I was trying to comfort the poor idiot. She was the silliest
of women and she bored the pants off me, but I did feel that
she had been badly treated. Even as I spoke, however, I was
discomfited by the realization of how fatuous I was being.
Obviously I had read the offending column and she had
read it. I knew as well that they took daily delivery on the
rag. I had seen it day after day on the Gibbons' doorstep.
There were other neighbors who took it as well but only as
an adjunct to some more decent news source. For Lollypop
and Tootsie Roll Gibbons, this seemed to be their only
newspaper. I wasn't ready to speak for the oaf they had
spawned. I was inclined to think the boy couldn't read. I felt
certain that even if he could, he wouldn't.

To get back to Lolly, however, if I had to visualize the
sort of reader who would be the hard-core aficionado of that
society page, I would automatically picture something in

the guise of Lollypop Gibbons. My words should have been no comfort to her, but they were.

"Yes, Georgie," she said. "You're right. I know you're right, but still it's not pleasant to think of all those common, stupid people that do read it and they see this and they're laughing at us." She turned her pout on the windows across the garden. "That damn old witch," she said. "She tried to make fools of all of us, and, if you read that thing, you could think she'd succeeded."

You may have noticed that she called me Georgie. She's the only person I've ever known who did. I suppose it's one of the things I've always held against her. Even though I had from the first with that Gibbons tribe taken the greatest care lest proximity grow into intimacy, she had almost from the first fastened that Georgie on me. I'm certain it was only my carefully preserved aloofness that prevented it from growing into Georgie Porgie.

She went on and on with it. She didn't ask me how I came to have the paper or how I'd happened to read the offending column. She was too busy with an effort to detach herself from those lower orders I had indicated would be its only readers. She explained that they took the paper but not for themselves. It was one of the things they had to do for the couple they had working for them.

"All that you have to do these days to keep help," she wailed. "It's awful and it's getting worse all the time. They read it. They can't be without it, and you can imagine how it makes me feel, Georgie. It's horrid knowing that your servants are laughing at you."

I could see that saying that made her feel much better. She had established her position. With her next words she destroyed it. Daphne Hobbes might be thinking that she was riding high, but she would soon find out.

"She's riding for a fall, that one is," Lolly told me. "Daddy is seeing our lawyer and she's going to be sorry."

Enlarging on the sins of our neighbor across the garden, she made it clear that in her opinion they were made far more heinous by the fact that the lady was a foreigner.

"If she doesn't like it here, she can go right back where she came from. Who needs her? These foreigners—they come over here. We take them in. We treat them just like they belonged. We welcome them. We give them all our freedoms and all our comforts. They come over here to be freeloaders on the best standard of living the world has ever known. Do they appreciate it? Are they grateful? All they do is criticize. If they don't like it here, why do they keep coming? Why do they stay?"

The whole tirade could have been direct quotation from one of the hardy perennials of that paper's editorial page. If she never read the thing, then it had to be that she was depending on that couple she had working for her not only for the standard services but also for all her attitudes and opinions.

Coming down with a sudden need to be at my typewriter, I managed to shake loose from her. I had been determined that the first time I could catch her at home I was going to pin Jill Armitage down and make her come across the garden with me to set my friend Daphne straight on the gossip column's source.

As it happened, I didn't see her for the better part of a week. By the time I did catch up with her, I had simmered down and begun to forget the whole silly episode. In any event, I would still have wanted her to set Daphne straight but by then there was no longer any need. Jill had already taken care of it. She was not letting fall to me any of the credit for her accomplishments, especially since she had contrived to wring for herself out of the episode something more tangible than credit.

For the first time since any of us had known her there had been a change in the Armitage domiciliary arrangements.

She had vacated her apartment to a tenant but this time without acquiring as adjunct to a husband another place to live. This time she moved out without marrying. If you are thinking that this time she was just shacked up with some man without having gone through any of the legal or religious formalities and that Bagby is making a big thing of the oversight, you can forget it. Jill Armitage had merely shifted her base across the garden and taken up residence in Daff Darling's guestroom.

Since on the strength of that report she had planted in the gossip column they had tumbled into a friendship that rendered them all but inseparable and since a most importunate tenant had turned up on Jill's doorstep to dangle before her a mouth-watering rent, Daff Darling had insisted that her dearest Gillian not pass up so splendid a financial opportunity. It was so much cozier being together than running back and forth across the garden all the time.

I can't say I was without reservations about this arrangement the two ladies had whipped up between them, but then it was no business of mine and they were both unreservedly happy about it. From Daphne I had it that she had taken Jill in because she found the younger woman refreshing, stimulating entertainment, unremitting fun. Jill, for her part, was making no pretense. She just loved the arrangement, and why not? All that lovely rent money for her pocket and with it free loading at a level beyond any grifter's dreams. A room and bath more luxuriously appointed than anything she had ever done for herself, better service than she had ever been able to hire, beautiful food, superb wines, unlimited liquor.

"And all of it for free," she crowed. "No demands on me. Nothing even expected of me."

She did sound grasping and I wondered about her talking that way in the presence of her hostess but I had to conclude that she knew what she was doing.

Daphne Hobbes loved it, every unsavory word of it. She doted on her dearest Gillian's honesty. Also, she was finding her house guest invaluable. Hadn't I noticed her new hairdo? Jill had put her on to a miraculous scissors-and-comb boy and he had cut her hair exactly like Jill's. Of course, hers was white and Jill's wasn't, but only in the best light was it possible to distinguish between Daphne's white hair and Jill's platinum rinse. They had also discovered that they were of a size. They could wear one the other's clothes and that was delicious fun. It was like being back at school and without being forced to eat parsnips.

Furthermore, it wasn't as though Jill's tenant was just anyone. He was a lovely man. Daphne had never met him. She hadn't even so much as laid eyes on him, but she knew. It was what he had done with the balcony.

The balcony she had in mind overhung the garden. In Jill's house the Gibbons family occupied the lower apartment, in that case a three-story job. The two upper floors Jill kept for her own occupancy or now for the occupancy of the lovely man. The balcony was attached to Jill's living room on the lower of her two floors, and, immediately on moving in, this tenant of hers had established on it a garden of his own. I had noticed. If one stepped out into the garden, one couldn't help but notice. Pots of tree roses in full flower had been installed up there and between them what amounted to an unbroken hedge of other flowering plants. The effect was lush and it was handsome. It had occurred to me that a new resident, unaccustomed to being looked in on, might have set it up as a screen against the scrutiny of his neighbors across the garden. The same result, however, could have been achieved far less tastefully. If he was depriving his neighbors of any view of himself, he was giving them instead something beautiful to look at. So on the basis of his balcony plantings alone Daphne Hobbes knew him to be a lovely man.

"Nobody with so much taste," she said, "nobody that knowledgeable about plants could not be worth knowing. I'm longing to meet him. We shall have to give a party."

Recalling the party that had been the beginning of all this, I wondered about how many of our garden group could be persuaded to attend another Daphne Hobbes bout of festivities. Possibly she had her own doubts. She evidently didn't consider it enough to ask people in to meet the new resident. She said she would have to find an occasion.

Only hours later she was provided with what she might well have considered her occasion. Anyone else would have been likely to take it as an occasion for going to the police, but not Daphne Hobbes. She had her own methods.

It happened during the night and it must have been deep in the night at an hour when every last one of us with windows on the garden would have been solidly asleep. I know that I heard nothing. I was, therefore, in no position to question the word of any of my neighbors when with unanimity they said that they likewise heard nothing.

In the morning, nevertheless, it was there. From my windows across the garden it was anything but obvious. Even when I had learned about it and was looking for it, from that distance I could make out only some of it.

In Daphne Hobbes' house looking out, however, or across the garden close up to her windows, there was no missing it. During the night every one of her garden windows had been holed through. Shots from an air rifle had been aimed at each of her windows in turn. Someone had been taking target practice by moonlight and someone was a crack shot. None of the window frames showed a mark. No brick of the house wall showed a chip or a dent. The marksman had aimed at glass and all up and down that garden facade he had hit wherever he aimed. He hadn't missed once.

When I looked across the garden before breakfast, I saw the crowd. What seemed to be at least half the neighbors were doing an inspection. I went out to join them. By the time I came along the whole lot was already working on Daphne. My first words did no more than echo what they had been telling her.

"This," I said, "is for the police."

"In my opinion," Daphne replied, "it is not, and I shall deal with it after my own fashion."

"It concerns all of us," I told her.

"I disagree," Daphne said.

"When it was the hawk," I reminded her, "you saw it as a collective concern."

"And that it was. This is different. This is directed at me alone. I shall give the young monkey's father ample opportunity to cope. If he doesn't cope or if he fails to cope satisfactorily, I shall then consult my solicitor."

"You can see how well he coped after the hawk thing," I argued.

I was not alone in the argument. Virtually all the neighbors were in there saying the same thing. There were only two exceptions, Jill Armitage and a man I didn't know. I could guess that the man would be Jill's tenant.

So far as I could tell, Jill was all for concurring with Dahpne in whatever course of action the lady chose to take. The hawk party had been too much fun. Jill seemed to be looking forward to more of the same. The man's reaction was more elemental.

"Am I right in thinking everybody knows who did it?" he asked.

Nobody was having the first doubt about who had done it. A dozen voices were raised to fill him in. Daphne's voice won out. We fell silent and left it to her to tell him. They were her windows.

She did a quick, clear, and concise job of it.

"It's obvious," she said in conclusion. "The lad's father disciplined him for shooting the hawk and it appears to be a lad who doesn't take well to discipline. He has revenged himself on me. We shall now see what the father does."

"The father doesn't even come across to look at the damage."

That was Mike Grassi. He was standing behind me, but I didn't have to look around to see who was speaking. I know Mike's growl. Mike is my landlord. Except for the ground floor he rents to me, he occupies the whole of the house himself. He needs all of the four stories for the Grassi brood. There are nine kids, all boys. Mike says he wanted a football team, but Clara—Clara's his wife—doesn't go for football. She says it's too rough, so Mike has had to settle for a baseball team.

"They're not at home," Daphne told him. "I rang over there and there's been no response. I gather that they are away and the lad, if he's there, knows it's the better part of wisdom not to answer."

Jill's tenant came back into it.

"I suppose I should be keeping my mouth shut," he said. "I'm new here and only on a rental, but it seems to me . . ."

Jill broke in on him to perform the introductions. She made a big formal thing of it. It could be that she had been taking protocol lessons from Daphne Hobbes. His name was Jackson.

"John Jackson," he said, volunteering the amplification of Jill's Mr. Jackson. "Call me Jack," he added. "Everybody does. Jack for John or short for Jackson. It doesn't matter. Either way it's Jack."

If all his word play drew from the crowd was a few titters, he was frank in his own enjoyment of it. He laughed and, even though the wit may have been feeble, the laugh was infectious. When a laugh has a good baritone timbre to it and when a laugh puts on display good white teeth and crinkles a man's face in lines of merriment, it does much to make you like the laugher.

I was having a first impression that said there might not be much we could expect from Jack Jackson in the way of bright conversation, but wit isn't all. Cheerful good nature and the beautification of Jill's balcony were items worth tossing into the account.

He was a pleasant-looking man. Of no more than medium height, he had good shoulders, a narrow waist, and the easy carriage of the natural athlete. His hair had begun going gray but he was to such an extent without any other signs of even the beginnings of middle age that I was inclined to guess that the graying was premature and that he was no older than Mike Grassi, who, for all the nine kids, had yet to see his thirty-fifth birthday.

Daphne waited until everyone's name had been tossed around. Once that was out of the way, she invited our new neighbor to finish what he'd been saying.

"Since you know who's doing it," he said, "there's no reason for bringing the police into it. This is the kind of thing his old man has to take care of out in the woodshed." He broke off briefly to let us have another of those winning laughs. "Living in the city," he continued, "you're at a disadvantage. You don't have woodsheds, but if that was my kid, I wouldn't let a little thing like that stop me."

Daphne beamed at the man. Predisposed in his favor because of his taste in plants, she now was completely taken with him because of what she took to be the soundness of his reasoning.

"My thinking precisely," she said.

"If it was a question of finding out who did it," Jackson added, "then there might be some reason for bringing the police in on it. That's the kind of operation they're tooled up for, finding the culprit. This is different. It's just a matter of discipline and, if his father isn't man enough for it, there's plenty of us here who are. We can draw lots for it."

I was letting that one go by. It just couldn't be a serious

suggestion. Looking around at the men gathered there in the garden, I could see that, just as I was doing, they were all shoving the thought aside, even if regretfully. Mike was the one who spoke for all of us.

"That's all right if you want to dream," he said, "but you can't go around hitting other people's kids."

"Who says we can't?" Jackson blustered. "I can, and, given half a chance, I will."

"Then, Mr. Jackson, you better know this right now," Mike told him. "I've got nine boys and anyone touches a one of them, I'll break his arm. So maybe you better watch that stuff."

"You and who else?"

You may be finding this hard to believe. I heard it and I asked myself if he could actually be saying it or could possibly be meaning it; but there they were, Mike Grassi and this new neighbor, just about ready to square off. I hadn't seen anything like it since way back in the days when my voice was changing.

Someone had to create a diversion and there wasn't any reason why I shouldn't be the one to do it. Anyhow I had something I thought needed saying and there was never going to be a better time for saying it.

I turned to Daphne. "Since you're not calling the police," I said, "I shall."

"No," Daphne insisted. "I am grateful for your solicitude, but this is my affair and I shall deal with it as I see fit and with interference from nobody. I do not like meddling, no matter how well intentioned."

I was prepared for that. I had expected something of the sort. I knew Daphne Hobbes well enough.

"I'm a timid type," I said. "Tonight it might be my windows, and I have a hot-tempered landlord."

I also know Mike Grassi. The last of that got to him. He

grinned and his fists unclenched. I can claim no equal success with Daphne Hobbes.

"Timid, my foot," she scoffed. "The situations you waltz into with your Inspector Schmidt."

"Never unnecessarily," I told her. "Only when there's no help for it."

She shrugged. "Of course," she said, "I can hardly stop you calling the police. But you must know I very much dislike telling lies and it would be a kindness if you just refrained from putting me in the position where I shall be forced to lie."

"Forced to lie? I don't understand."

I didn't. She had me stopped cold.

"If the police come into it," she explained, "I shall tell them I did it myself. I shot the holes in my windows on a whim. The police will understand. After all, I am English and we English do have a reputation for eccentricity. Daft as a brush, all of us, the whole silly nation."

She was a woman used to having her own way and she was skilled in the processes of getting it. Jill Armitage loved it. She laughed her silly head off.

"Daff darling, you are a bloody marvel," she gurgled.

You could see that, along with the other goodies, she was also picking up language from her friend.

The rest of the assembled neighbors merely smiled or at the most they chuckled, but right through the group I could sense the relief. They had none of them felt they could decently stay uninvolved but, with the possible exception of our new neighbor, Jack Jackson, they were none of them people who would welcome involvement. Jackson might have been contemplating the removal of those balcony plants Daphne so much admired and their replacement with a balcony woodshed, but all the others were obviously ready to leave it that they had done their best and the redoubtable Mrs. Hobbes had taken the matter out of their hands.

I could have told her that if it came to the place where she would feel she had to put the thing in the hands of her lawyer, that worthy wouldn't thank her for having put such a lie on record with the police. She would have left him with no ground to stand on. I didn't bother. It would have been an exercise in futility. She would have considered it a little thing, and little things never gave Daphne Hobbes pause.

Me, however, it did give pause. I hadn't the first doubt that she would do precisely as she said. Daphne was a woman of her word and I was left with no place to go. If I did make the call, her lie would put me in the position of having accomplished nothing beyond wasting the time of the always-overburdened police. Furthermore, because of me, she would have put herself in the position of having cut herself off from any sort of legal recourse.

I happened to be seeing Inspector Schmidt that day—not on any of this, of course, but on other matters—and I mentioned it to him. He took Daphne's side of the argument.

"The boy's folks'll know she could have called the precinct and she didn't," he said. "They're likely to appreciate that and it'll make for better relations the way you all live over there, everyone under everybody else's eye all the time. There's another thing, too. Parents have them a lug like this Gibbons kid, they think a brush with the police is bothering him as much as it bothers them. So it ends up with their deciding the kid's been punished enough and they don't do anything much about him. Her way, it puts the whole package in his old man's lap. He'll have to do something about straightening Junior around."

"He doesn't seem to have done much straightening around after the brat shot the hawk," I observed.

Schmitty shrugged it off. "So your Mr. Gibbons doesn't have the best attitude toward the ecology bit," he said. "And the way this English dame handled that, she made the boy's folks so angry at her that it had to take the edge off what they felt about sonny boy. This is different. Papa finds himself stuck with paying for all that window glass and at today's prices. It's not the same as a bird that didn't cost him a dime."

The inspector had a point. We moved on to talk about other things. That afternoon when I got back home, it did look as though Schmitty was right and Daphne Hobbes had pursued the best possible course. I didn't for a moment think she had taken this course for any of those good reasons Schmitty had lined out for me, but, whatever her reasons, the thing did seem to be working itself out.

The house opposite was aswarm with workmen. They seemed to be all over the place, taking damaged glass out, putting new glass in. Daddy Gibbons was also over there, giving the job his personal supervision.

It's all right for you to be impressed by that, but don't be overimpressed. Don't let it knock you over. This happened to be a Saturday. Tootsie Roll wasn't taking time off from his office. At most it might have been time off from golf or from watching a ball game. Since it was Saturday, Mike Grassi was also around, or at least he came in shortly after I did. He'd had all his nine boys over to the park, all the way from the thirteen-year-old firstborn down to the one-year-old carriage trade.

Clara took over on the tribe and Mike dropped in for a quick one with me. He's likely to do that at times like this when he's fresh from running his youngsters around. Clara commandeers one of their bathrooms for bathing the sweat and grime off the little ones and she distributes the bigger boys over their other bathrooms to get themselves showered. It leaves Mike waiting till there will be a bathroom clear for his own shower. I like the guy, even when he's sweaty, and since it always comes at drink time, it's become something of a pattern.

Having the ground floor, I, of course, have direct access to the garden. In a house which hadn't been divided into apartments—the one Daphne Hobbes had, for example—access to the garden was the same as mine. She could walk right out. In most of the houses—mine, where Mike Grassi had me as a tenant of the ground-floor apartment; Jill's, next door, where the lower floors were rented to Gibbons; and all the houses that had been split up into apartments—wrought-iron, elaborately caged, spiral staircases had been tacked onto the outside walls on the garden side to afford the upstairs people a way down into the garden. It was an accepted thing that Mike would come trotting down his spiral and pop in on me.

He could also come into my place without going outside. We were so easy with each other that for years I had taken to leaving my apartment door unlocked. There was a good lock on the street door. Anyone who got past that one with burglary in mind would have no trouble with the locks Mike and I had on the doors between our places and our common hall. In bad weather, if Mike wanted to drop in on me he could do it without going out into the cold or wet. Also, anytime when his boys were being boys and he'd brought work home from the office, he was free to drop down to my place and bring his work with him. It didn't matter whether I was in or out. You could do that sort of thing with Mike. He was that sort of guy. Also, the traffic went both ways. I would go up and drop in on them anytime I felt like it.

So we sat with our Virginia Gentleman—rocks for Mike and water for me—and we watched the action across the garden. Mike was loving it. That afternoon he could have been the world's happiest man. He filled me in and he enjoyed every word of it.

"You know Mrs. Hobbes got to Gibbons the minute he

came in," Mike explained. "You must have heard them work on Eric, trying to get him to admit it, the way they were screaming at him all morning. It's never stopped. You can hear them now. With Tootsie Roll over there, it's Lollypop having her innings. Eric is still lying up, down, and sideways. He swears he didn't do it, but Gibbons didn't hesitate even for a minute. He's not only paying for all that glass. He's also paying Saturday overtime and for extra men, too."

"I can just see Daphne demanding that," I murmured. "She wouldn't wait over the weekend or hold still for letting the work be stretched out."

Mike laughed. He was inordinately gleeful about the whole thing.

"Mrs. Hobbes might have been ready to demand it," he said. "We'll never know. She didn't have to demand anything. It was all Gibbons' idea and, boy, is it ever costing him!"

I grimaced. I was beginning to find Mike's joy distasteful. Gibbons had never been one of my favorite people, but the poor man did have problems. With that wife and that son, he had them up to his ears. At the moment, furthermore, I couldn't see where anyone could fault him. He was going all out to repair the damage and to all appearances he was doing it with good grace.

"I can be sorry for the dope," I said.

"I can't," Mike told me. "He's a menace."

"Eric, yes. I'd be sorry for you if you had one like that."

"They're a menace, the whole damn family," Mike insisted. "They scare me. They scare me for my kids. You know how kids are. The little ones learn from the big ones, and if there's anything bad to learn, that's just the thing they do learn. Do you think we sleep easy, Clara and me, with them right next door and Eric around for ours maybe to learn from?"

I had to laugh at him. "You don't look scared," I said.

"You look too sadistically happy. What's with you, Mike? You've never been a vindictive guy."

Mike grinned. "You think I'm enjoying the way it's costing Gibbons?" he said. "The cost is only temporary. He's taking it out of Eric's allowance and for however long it will take Eric to pay it off. Maybe that's why it's this spare-no-expense deal. It's costing Eric, and he's fixing it for it to cost the kid plenty. There's a boy who's going to be broke for one hell of a long time, much too broke to be buying any ammo."

"I'd take his guns away from him," I said. "I'd do that just for starters."

"Me too," Mike agreed. "Gibbons has other ideas."

"So has our new neighbor, Jackson," I said.

"That big noise. Mr. You-and-who-else." Mike had no time for Jackson. He went on about Gibbons. "If Eric is so addicted to guns," Mike said, "it's his old man's idea to send him some place where he'll learn gun manners."

"Like where?"

"Military school. It goes back to that day Mrs. Hobbes shoved the hawk at Lollypop. Tootsie Roll started checking out military schools then and he's got one lined up. Eric goes in the fall, as soon as the new term starts."

"And that's the news that makes you a bundle of joy?" I said.

"You're damn tootin' it is. Only a couple of months of worrying about the effect he can be having on my kids, and then it's summer and I can stop worrying."

I knew what he meant. Clara and the kids were always away during the summer months. One pair of grandparents had a place somewhere in the mountains and the other pair lived at the shore. Each got Clara and the nine grandsons for half the summer and Mike stayed in town alone except for joining them on weekends. By the time they would be returning to town, the Eric menace would have been removed. He would be off learning gun manners.

It did seem as though all problems were well in hand.

That night when the sound woke me, I woke to the thought that I'd heard a shot. Simultaneously with having the thought, however, I put it aside. I felt certain that I had only been dreaming a shot. What could have been more natural than that on this night I should have been dreaming gunfire?

I wasn't left to delude myself for long. It wasn't more than a few moments before Daphne Hobbes screamed and in no time at all lights came up all around the garden and we came puring out of our houses and apartments in pajamas, robes, and slippers, or at the most in hastily hauled-on shirts and pants.

Daphne Hobbes screamed and screamed and screamed, but Jill Armitage was silent. Jill lay on Daphne's living-room floor. She had been shot through the head and it was obvious that the shot had been instantly fatal. Her body lay by the bar and I had to force myself away from the thought that Daphne was too far gone in hysteria to put Jill on a paper plate and pop her into the bar freezer.

III

And that is how Inspector Schmidt came to know my neighbors. You may be thinking that this was just the sort of open-and-shut-job that could have been left to the detective squad attached to our local precinct, nothing that could call for the intervention of the inspector's expertise. Even at first sight, however, I had some doubts about it. What all the others around the garden were accepting as the obvious just didn't seem all that obvious to me.

I called Schmitty. "It could be the Gibbons boy," I told him. "He is the complete lout and he's evidently a great marksman. The hawk could have been a lucky shot, but just last night popping every one of those windows without even one shot going astray—that was a convincing exhibition of marksmanship. And now we have this. She was drilled right through the head. Everything says it was the Gibbons boy and he just got the wrong woman, but I don't know. There's just enough doubt, Schmitty. Want to take your own look at it?"

"Doubt, Baggy?" the inspector asked. "When you were telling me about the kid and the windows earlier today, you weren't having any doubts."

"That was earlier. Then it all added up. Mrs. Hobbes raised a fuss about the hawk. Mrs. Hobbes got him in trouble. He got even with Mrs. Hobbes by popping all her windows."

"And that got him in worse trouble," Schmitty said, picking it up from me. "So now he's even with her and for good, except that he got the wrong woman."

"That's it," I said. "Why the wrong woman? Is she the wrong woman?"

"Isn't that what you said? The wrong woman?"

"The wrong woman for young Eric," I explained. "I can't imagine the boy giving a hoot in hell about the nastiness of that newspaper story. It drew blood, Schmitty, but not from the boy—from his mother and father."

The inspector laughed. "Take a good hard look at what you're suggesting, Baggy boy," he said. "Mom and pop are mad at her because she made fools of them in the paper. They fix her for it with a slug through the head. It's real handy for them, a murder they can get away with because their one and only son is the one who'll take the rap for it. They're in the clear, and after all, Eric is a juvenile. So it won't be too bad a rap. Is that the way parents play it over where you live?"

As you already know, I held no exalted opinion of Lollypop and Tootsie Roll but, of course, Schmitty was right. There was no way I could believe that of them. It was easier to imagine that a parent, saddled with a son the like of Eric Gibbons, could pick up a gun and shoot the oaf than to picture a parent planning a murder in the expectation that he can get off by putting it on his son.

"Not that way," I said. "Not in any such simple setup, but suppose it's been rigged so nothing can be proved on the boy."

Schmitty would have none of it. "Still not the kind of chance any father or mother is going to take," he said. "The motive for the killing is thin in the first place, and, even if nothing can be proved and the kid does get off, he'll have gone through the wringer anyhow and that's too much for any parent to set up for his kid. Still, none of that means you haven't got something. I'll drop over."

And that's Inspector Schmidt for you. He had only just finished doing a total job on demolishing every nebulous idea I'd had chasing around in my head and he turns about and tells me I do have something after all. While I waited for him to drop around, I kept wondering what it could be that I did have. So far as I could figure it, Schmitty had left me with nothing.

Meanwhile, the precinct men were at work across the garden and they destroyed even that small doubt that had pushed me off on my crazy line of thinking. They established something that I hadn't known. The negligee Jill had been wearing, the one that was still draped about her inert body, wasn't one of her own. It belonged to Daphne Hobbes. Jill had spilled tea on hers that evening and had borrowed one of Daphne's.

I wondered what I was going to say to the inspector when he did turn up. It seemed to me that this one fact straightened out the whole thing. The victim was the wrong woman and the mistake seemed obvious. The killer had recognized the negligee and he had been misled by it.

There could be some question about how the killer would have recognized the negligee as Daphne's when I had not. Obviously nobody had been occupying an observation point superior to mine, but that question didn't trouble me for long. I found the answer to it too obvious.

I hadn't been sitting up nights concentrating on the house across the garden and watching for a good chance to get off a shot at Daphne Hobbes. According to her account, she had several of those negligees, all of them alike except for color. Habitually in the course of the night she would have a period of wakefulness and she always armed herself for those times by keeping an assortment of books on her bedside table so that she could read herself back to sleep.

"I have this odd difficulty," she was telling the precinct boys. "I never seem able to judge just what sort of thing I am going to want to read. Virtually every night I do this same stupid thing. I wake and in all that assortment of books I've prepared for just such a moment I haven't a thing that seems at all suitable. So night after night I get up and shrug into a negligee and go downstairs and switch on lights and prowl the bookshelves for the one book I've come to want."

Just a few words about the geography of the room where Jill Armitage died and another few words about Jill, and the whole picture will come as clear for you as it did for me. The bookshelves were in an alcove. Anyone prowling the shelves for a book would not be on view through the garden windows. Only in her passage through the room, coming to and going from the book alcove, would Daphne Hobbes have been seen, and then only deep in the room, on the move, and never in a position where she would have offered an easy target.

If Jill Armitage had shrugged into that negligee and come downstairs for a book, she would probably have been all right, and it's not because I write books and am trying to promote sales that I'm saying it. Jill had come down for a snort and Daphne's bar is not set back out of sight in any alcove. Going to the bar, she presented the best target that the killer was ever likely to have. You can see how he would have hurried to take advantage of it, especially if he had been many nights waiting for a good line of fire.

This information about the negligee wasn't the only thing I had to catch up on. At the beginning I had stopped only for a quick look at the body before running back across the garden to phone the inspector. When I returned after talking with him, I was too taken up with what Daphne was saying to take much notice of anything else. Mike had taken notice and he was steaming.

He grabbed hold of my arm and whispered. He was so tense that he was unaware of the savagery he was putting into his grip. I was aware. It was my arm and I felt it. Looking down at his hand, I could see the whitening of his knuckles.

"It's not a thing anyone can want to do," he groaned. "Just thinking of doing it has me hating myself, but somebody'll have to speak. He's not going to come out."

I looked around me and immediately saw what was eating on him. We were all there, at least one of us out of every house and apartment around the garden, but with the one conspicuous exception. There was no Gibbons among us, not Eric, not his father, not his mother. I would like to have thought that they were sound sleepers and that nothing had wakened them, not the shot, not Daphne's screams, none of the ensuing hubbub. I couldn't think it. It was clearly not the case. They weren't even trying to make a pretense of it. Lights were showing in all their windows. Looking over there, I couldn't see any of them in any of those lighted rooms, but I had a clear memory of something that I had seen. At the time of my seeing it, it had looked to be so natural that I'd let it pass without giving it any thought, but now it had become something to think about.

When I'd been running back across the garden to hit my telephone, I had seen lights over there. At that time it hadn't been all the windows, only those that gave on the bedrooms, but that had been enough to say they were awake. In the minutes since then, all those other lights had been turned on. Beyond question the Gibbons family was up and about.

Mike Grassi didn't want to speak. He was a father himself and you can see how even the thought of fingering a kid would have been tearing him up. I can't say I was happy about taking it on, but my situation was nothing like Mike's. I have no boys of my own. It doesn't keep me from feeling for kids, but I suppose the feeling would have to be at a lower level of intensity.

Also among all the neighbors I was the only one who had anything more than the standard, private citizen-police officer relationship with the precinct detectives of the job. Through my association with the inspector, I knew them and they knew me. Also, the inspector was on his way over. He would take it as par for the course if none of the others had volunteered the information to fill the boys in on what all of us had in our minds. He would take a dim view of any reticences I permitted myself. He had told me often enough that, working with him as I did, I was something like half a cop. That all too frequently he had the feeling that I was the less useful half made no difference. The fraction was still there.

I allowed myself the small luxury of making a choice. I picked Luis Garcia. He was young, not so far away from it himself that he could have forgotten what it's like to be a teenager. He was tough, quite tough enough to do what had to be done and to do it right. He was also gentle and sensitive. My neighbors, like them or not, were in a rough enough spot. Nobody had to go to any extra lengths to give them a hard time.

I shook Mike off.

"Let me handle it," I told him. "The inspector's on the way over and I know these precinct men."

"Inspector Schmidt?" Mike was startled. "I thought he came on only for the tough ones, not an open-and-shut thing like this."

"Yes," I said. "But I'm here. My friends are involved and I'm a big shot. I rate nothing less than the inspector himself."

I wanted to relax him if only a little. It's no fun watching a man work on an ulcer.

I barged in on Garcia and buttonholed him.

"Look, Lou," I said. "I just talked to the inspector. He's on his way over, but he'd want me to fill you in."

"You've got something, sir?"

It's only manners, but Lou Garcia is the kind of young cop who invariably makes me feel a couple of hundred years old. I try to tell myself it's only Inspector Schmidt's departmental eminence that has rubbed off on me.

"Background," I told him. "What everybody's thinking and nobody has the stomach to say."

I gave him a quick rundown on our previous shooting episodes and the action that had been taken on them.

"Everyone else is out here," I said. "Only the kid and his father and mother haven't surfaced. Everyone else but the young kids. It could be nothing more than embarrassment. Coming out and facing the neighbors could take a lot of doing; but, without making any accusations, I can't help thinking they could be hard at work over there monkeying with evidence."

Lou nodded. "It can't hurt anything if I go over," he said. "You know, just question them on what maybe they heard or saw. Like we'll need all the witnesses we can line up."

"The name is Gibbons, William Gibbons. The boy is Eric."

"You know them?"

"Neighbors."

"They know about the way you work with the inspector?"

"They know."

"Then only if you don't mind, maybe you'll come over with me and introduce me like. I'm just thinking we can maybe get more that way than if it's like 'Police. Open up.'"

I didn't know whether I minded or not. Curiosity was pulling me one way. Revulsion against intruding myself on people to watch them when they might be touching bottom exerted an equal pull the other way.

There was a third factor, however, and it tipped the balance. I can't say that at this stage of the thing I had any notion that it could come to this, that I would be writing this account of the shootings. I wasn't seeing the thing as shaping up into anything that could be an Inspector Schmidt case, but even as it stood then, it did seem to me to have aspects that made it peculiar enough to set it up as the makings of a short piece for one of the magazines.

So there it was. I was thinking it could develop into good copy even though not a Schmidt story. After all, I was there. I was in on the ground floor. Crime writing is my business. I could hardly walk away from it.

"Okay, Lou," I said. "Let's go."

Mike Grassi watched us start across the garden. I could read his look of sympathy.

"Rather you than me, my friend," it was telling me. "Sorry if I'm the one who got you into this."

We had gone no farther than would indicate where we were headed when Jack Jackson came hurrying after us.

"How's to take along some help," he offered. "That's one big hunk of boy. A lot of muscle on him. Could be he'll take a lot of handling."

"Thanks," Lou said, "but no. I'll be all right, sir, and it's better with civilians out of it."

Jerking his head in my direction, Jackson cocked an eyebrow at me. Tacitly, he was asking the question:

"Since when is he a cop? He's just the guy next door."

"Mr. Bagby," he said, "has been working with the police on murder investigations for a lot longer than I've been on the force. He's had experience. He knows the routine we have to follow."

Jackson's lip curled. "I know," he said, "reading them their rights and all that crap. I know the routine that ought to be followed. I'd be glad to pay for the rope."

Straight out of some old Western dug up for TV. Lou looked as though he might be about to ask if the man was for real. He controlled it.

"That's something you'd have to take up with the Supreme Court, sir," Lou told him, and we went across the garden, leaving Jackson to the enjoyment of his law-and-order outrage.

I knocked at the Gibbons' garden door. Through the glass we could see into the room. It was bright with light but there was no one in it. We waited, but no one came. We were getting no response to my knock. Lou tried and he put a lot more knuckle into it. It did no good. Nobody came.

I tried the door and was startled to find it locked. I wasn't prepared to say that for the Gibbons family locking their garden door was an act without precedent. I had all along carefully avoided coming to anything like drop-in terms with that trio. I therefore had no knowledge of what they did about their garden door, but I did know that I never locked mine. Daphne Hobbes never locked hers. I had never known any of the ground-floor people to lock their garden doors. Upstairs people as well were in the habit of leaving the doors to their garden spirals unlocked. I knew that the Grassis always did, and so did Jill Armitage.

There's no access to the garden except by way of the houses, and hadn't we always been one happy family? Like all other New Yorkers, we did secure ourselves from the outside world, but not back there among ourselves, not against our little community of garden neighbors.

If, as I had assumed it would be, the door had been unlocked, I don't know whether Lou would have wanted to go barging in, but obviously he had no intention of breaking the door down. He was looking for a bell.

I told him there wasn't any.

"Out front," I said, "at the street entrance. There are bells out there. Want to go around and ring?"

"Looks like the way to do it."

"I'm right next door," I said, leading the way. "We can go through my place."

My garden door was standing ajar. I hadn't bothered to shut it behind me when I'd first gone across the garden or again when I'd come out after phoning Inspector Schmidt. I noticed that virtually all my neighbors had likewise left theirs standing open. Rushing out to investigate a shot and screams, one is hardly likely to stop to shut doors carefully behind one, not when the doors open on nothing more public than our enclosed garden and not when it is a balmy and rainless spring night.

As we came in, Lou moved to shut my door behind us.

"Leave it," I said. "It's a fine night."

"Don't you want it locked?"

"It doesn't go anywhere any strangers can get to," I said. "Nobody ever locks up back here."

"Except now tonight your next-door neighbor," Lou muttered.

I didn't want to be giving him any ideas when I was myself not certain. As we went through my place to go out to the street, I explained that for their door I couldn't say it was only this one night. Not having been in the habit of popping in on them, for all I could know that door of theirs might always have been locked.

"They've never really been part of the crowd," I explained, "except in a surface way. We're all together here, so we can't exclude anybody or build any open hostilities. It's just that everyone else is at least someone's special buddy. They're nobody's buddy."

We went out to the street. If Lou Garcia had been concerned about what might have seemed my too-cavalier attitude toward security, it undoubtedly made him feel better when he saw the care with which I did lock the street door behind us.

Seen from the street, the Gibbons place confronted me with a fresh astonishment. I've already told you that all the rooms with garden windows had been ablaze with light. So now I was seeing that the same went for all the rooms with windows on the street side of the building. Here, however, there was a difference. Here the rooms were not only full of light. Here they were not empty of people.

From the street, of course, you couldn't see in through any of the windows. I've told you about the way we're set up, open to the garden but well screened from the view of anyone passing on the street side. What we could see, however, were shadows on the window blinds. On bulk I could identify these shadows—Gibbons, Flora, Eric. I am prepared to guarantee that it was not my imagination that made them look like agitated shadows. They scurried back and forth across the window blinds.

"Too busy in this end of the place to hear a knock," I said, "or too much they have to do before they can answer one."

Lou rang the bell. You could have thought the Gibbonses were hooked in on their bell wiring. The shadows froze. For a moment after Lou's finger came away from the button they remained frozen, but it was only a moment and then they moved again. The three shadows clumped together and only when Lou tried the bell again did they come unstuck. That second ring broke them apart. Two receded and disappeared. One—I could tell from the shape and size that it was Bill Gibbons—passed across the screened windows. He was coming to answer Lou's ring.

I can't pretend I had ever liked the man. I'd found him less repulsive than his wife or his son but never to the point of building anything but the coolest feeling toward him. Seeing him now, however, the way he was when he opened the door, made me sick with pity for the poor idiot. White and haggard, he looked as though his blood, bleached out to colorlessness, was oozing out of him disguised as sweat.

He didn't wait for any questions. He didn't even wait for us to speak, much less give me the moment it would have taken to introduce Detective Garcia. He knew about the work I did with the inspector. To his way of thinking, I had always been something in the nature of quasi-police. It's a conclusion people are likely to jump to. They assume that I am not even half as quasi as is the actual fact.

So this neighbor, who is a policeman of sorts and specifically one who is mostly concerned with murder, comes to his door fresh on the heels of a shooting and brings with him a stranger who has poised at the doorbell a finger that gives every appearance of being authority-laden. Even as stupid a lug as was this Tootsie Roll couldn't have failed to make a lightning-flash reading on who it would be I had brought to call on him.

"No," he shouted. "Not this time." Hearing himself, he recognized that he was screaming. He paused and swallowed. It was a convulsive swallow. If you don't know what I mean when I tell you that I could see the desperation of it in the way his Adam's apple moved and his throat muscles worked, then you have never seen a man when he is under unendurable stress and is fighting to bring his voice under control. He didn't quite make it. He brought it down but he couldn't adjust it to any normal level. It dropped to a husky whisper. "The boy was asleep," he said. "He slept through it all, the rifle shot, the screaming. I had to wake him. And last night, too, when he said he didn't, I should have believed him. He wasn't lying then. I know that now, because he isn't lying now."

I should have sensed something from the movement of the man's eyes. In the middle of what he was saying his gaze shifted from looking at Lou and me to looking past us. I did notice it but I had been taking it to mean that he couldn't say what he was saying and go on looking us in the eye. A man will often do that when he is lying or even being evasive. He will look past you, fixing his gaze on empty space.

So when Inspector Schmidt spoke from just over my shoulder, I jumped. I hadn't heard his car pull in and I hadn't heard him come up behind me. There was no need to introduce him. Obviously Gibbons knew who he was. The inspector had been around my place often enough for the neighbors to recognize him on sight.

"Could we take this inside?" Schmitty said. "Or are we putting on a show for the whole neighborhood?"

All the time Lou had been working on the doorbell, the street had been locked in its nighttime silence. The shot back in our garden, if it had sounded in the street at all, would have been only a small noise out there, and Daphne's screams had most likely not carried this far. The police cars that had swarmed over from the precinct had all gone to the Hobbes address and that naturally had taken them into the parallel street to the north of this one. A cordon had been thrown around all the houses that had access to the garden, but the precinct men on that duty had come around from the other street and had come on foot and quietly. Inspector Schmidt's car, coming to my address, had been the first police car to arrive on this side of our houses and he hadn't been riding his siren.

Now that he had spoken of the neighborhood, I looked behind me. The street was no longer solidly asleep. Lights had come up in several windows across from us and, even as I looked, they were coming up in additional windows. People over there were leaning out, watching and listening. Obviously Gibbons' shouting had roused them.

"Inspector Schmidt?" Gibbons asked.

It was the strangled whisper again but now so much tamped down that it was only barely audible. It could have been largely by lip reading that I knew he had spoken the inspector's name.

"We can talk better inside, Mr. Gibbons," Schmitty said.

I could see how he knew. I had filled him in on the target practice of the night before and on the way Gibbons had reacted to that. For Schmitty to have pieced that together with what Gibbons had said in that moment when Gibbons had been speaking as much to the inspector as to Lou Gar-

cia and me was no remarkable feat. For Inspector Schmidt it
had to be all too easy.

Gibbons hesitated. He took a long look at his audience in
the windows across the street. I guess what he saw there decided him. He drew back out of the doorway, making way
for us to come in. Then he slammed the door shut behind us.
It was a violent slam but it did him no good. It brought him
no release from his agony and tension.

Inside he stood irresolute. He looked down at his hands.
It was as though he might be thinking that an intimidating
glare could make them behave. They didn't leave off their
shaking. Belatedly he hurried them into concealment in the
deep pockets of his silk robe. That wasn't much good either.
It was a thin robe. The silk shivered with the trembling of
his hands.

We were still not in his apartment. We were in the common hall he shared with the upstairs flat, the duplex which
had been Jill Armitage's and in which just then Jack Jackson
was the tenant in residence.

"Do you want to talk out here, Mr. Gibbons?" the inspector asked.

Gibbons was in no shape for knowing what he wanted. I
could see that he wasn't eager to take us into his place, but
then he didn't like it where we were either. He shot a trou-
bled glance toward the stairs. He didn't know whether Jackson would be up there or across the garden and, since he
didn't know, he opened his apartment door to us and let us
into the kitchen.

This was the room where he and his wife and son had been
doing all that scurrying around before wife and son faded
off and Tootsie Roll answered the doorbell. It was, of course,
an odd place to choose for settling in with us, but think of
the alternatives. A bathroom? A storeroom? Anything else
would be one of the rooms with garden windows and all of
our little world out in the garden to look in on him. I did

think of the bedrooms. Although they were on the garden side they did have shades that could and would be drawn, but I was guessing that it had been to the bedrooms that he had dispatched Lollypop and Eric before he went to the door. He would want to keep us away from them.

A couple of the kitchen cupboard doors stood open. If the tumbled mess of pots and pans and other utensils those cupboards contained was any token of the sort of housekeeping the couple they had working for them was providing, they were being gypped. Gibbons spotted the doors and hurried across the kitchen to push them shut.

It seemed a peculiar time for the man to be that much preoccupied with tidiness.

IV

"Now you were saying, Mr. Gibbons," Schmitty reminded him.

Gibbons took a deep breath. Just that small interval of moving about had given him the chance to take something of a grip on himself. When he spoke now, it was still not in his normal voice but he did sound steadier.

"I was telling George, Inspector, and this officer he brought over here with him, I was telling them that I knew that now everybody would be trying to put this thing onto my boy the same way as they did this morning," Tootsie Roll said. "You don't know what's been going on around here, but they've all got it in for my Eric."

Schmitty smiled at him. It was a friendly smile, indication that Inspector Schmidt was relaxed and suggesting to Gibbons that he could relax as well.

"If it is as you say," he told Gibbons, "then I'll be hearing the accusations soon enough. Let's have your side of it."

"The boy has been misunderstood." Gibbons jumped at the chance to speak up for his loutish Eric. "He's a good boy. He gets into mischief sometimes, but what boy doesn't? It's natural. Boys will be boys."

He was falling into cliché but that wasn't unlike him. He had never impressed me with any originality and at a time like this a man can coast on clichés while he's trying to shape up what he had to say next.

Schmitty played along, being helpful.

"You don't want a boy to be too good. You worry about maybe he hasn't enough spirit in him."

"The boy likes shooting," Gibbons went on. "He's no crack shot but he wants to be. He wants to work at it. Now, shooting off his shotgun here in the middle of the city, that was wrong. Shooting at a bird out of season, that was wrong, though on that you have to understand that the boy didn't know it was this rare kind of hawk or whatever."

"He did all that?" Schmitty asked.

The inspector, of course, did know from what I'd told him earlier in the day, but he wanted to hear it from the boy's father in the father's own version of the story.

"He did," Gibbons said. "I've never denied it. I took the responsibility for it."

He gave the inspector a rundown on the hawk episode, but I noticed that he was careful to omit any mention of how he came to know that what Daphne Hobbes had called the splendid bird had been killed. No mention of Daphne or of her gruesome champagne bash and not a word about Jill Armitage or the gossip-column account of the party and of the greening of our little group.

"You never denied it," Schmitty said. "What about your son? Did he admit doing it?"

"Yes. He hadn't known it was wrong."

That answer came a little too quickly and Tootsie Roll put too much emphasis on it. I didn't for a moment believe him. People are prone to do that. They think that speaking with enough conviction can be the same as being convincing.

The inspector contented himself with digging into only part of the statement.

"He didn't know it was wrong? He goes after birds with a shotgun in the middle of the city and way out of hunting season and he didn't know it was wrong? Would you say you have a bright boy there, Mr. Gibbons?"

"He didn't know anything about this endangered-species

stuff. I wouldn't have known anything about that myself. If I'd seen it flying over, I'd have had no idea of what kind of a bird it was or anything like that."

"But he did know it wasn't the right season or the right place?" Schmitty persisted.

Gibbons scowled.

"I said he's a boy," he growled. "I told you he gets into mischief sometimes."

"Okay, okay," the inspector said, shutting that off. "You were saying something about this morning, a thing people put on the boy this morning. Tell me about that."

"I blame myself," Gibbons began.

"Boys will be boys," Schmitty reminded him.

Gibbons would have none of that even though the words were his own coming back at him.

"That's the easy answer," he said, managing somehow to sound disdainful. "The easy answer isn't always the best answer. In a thing like this it isn't even a good answer. In fact, it's the worst possible answer, because it's been manufactured. We were set up for jumping to that very conclusion and we just let ourselves be manipulated. We jumped. I blame myself for not knowing better."

"You do know better now?"

Tootsie Roll went to great pains in laying out his complicated argument, and I had to hand it to him. He did a masterful job of it. Eric shot the hawk. When his father confronted him with the dead bird, he did try to deny having done it, but he hadn't been able to make the denial stand up.

"We had a man-to-man talk," Gibbons said, "and he confessed. Then this morning . . ." Gibbons broke off and glanced at the kitchen clock. "I suppose it's yesterday morning now. Anyhow when we woke yesterday and there was a hole in every one of those windows across the way, everybody assumed it had to be Eric again. I assumed it like everyone else, and, when he denied it, I just thought we were going to have to have another man-to-man talk the first chance I'd have to take the time for it. I didn't believe the boy, and I was wrong."

He was choosing to say nothing about the man-to-boy yelling we'd been hearing all day.

"Let's break that up," Schmitty suggested. "Great target shooting on the windows of the house opposite, and everybody—you included—assumed it had to be your son's work. Why?"

"Because the bird was his doing, because that wasn't the first time he'd fired a gun in the garden even if it was the first time he'd fired at anything or hit anything or killed anything. The way things go around here, all it has to be is a door slammed or a car backfiring and everybody's sure right off that it's got to be Eric with his gun."

Schmitty turned to me. "You live next door," he said. "Would you accept that as a fair description of what you thought about last night's shooting?"

Since I'd told the inspector about that episode, he knew that Tootsie Roll was omitting from his account a major reason for our arrival at the unanimous assumption. Obviously he wanted Gibbons confronted with the part of the story the man was choosing not to tell. Inspector Schmidt was electing me to provide that confrontation.

I tried to do it tactfully. I couldn't help feeling sorry for the poor slob. He was a father and he was going through hell.

"Certainly," I said, "all the earlier shooting we knew the boy had done was an important factor in our thinking that any shooting done back there in the garden would have been done by Eric. But there was more to it than that. It wasn't just any windows in the row of houses across the garden. It was all the windows of the one house, those and no others. Since it was the house that belongs to Mrs. Hobbes and it was Mrs. Hobbes who found the dead hawk and raised a storm about it, it did seem that shooting at her windows had to be a childish act of revenge. She had found the hawk. She had made an issue of it. Because of her the boy had been punished. We had to think that it was a boy's idea of getting even. It would have been a silly sort of revenge, of course, one that was certain to hurt him more than it could possibly hurt her, but all too often boys are just that silly."

You can see that I did try, but this was a brutal business and there was no way of putting it that could make it less brutal. It didn't astonish me that Gibbons blew up at me.

"Go on," he snarled. "Go on. Why stop there? Go on and say the rest of it. I know what you're thinking."

The inspector stepped between us and took me off the hook. He'd had all he wanted from me.

"You tell us, Mr. Gibbons," he said. "Tell us what he's been thinking."

"He's thinking the boy's a complete idiot," Gibbons said.

From the first I'd known the kid, I'd never thought anything else of Eric Gibbons. I saw no reason, however, for stepping back into it. I could accomplish nothing by either affirming or denying.

Gibbons went on with it. "He thinks that since I swept aside the boy's denials and since for the shooting at the windows I was putting on him a punishment far heavier than he'd had for killing the hawk, the boy could be so stupid that he would go for even more drastic revenge. He would actually take a shot at the Hobbes woman."

"I suppose he denies it," Inspector Schmidt said.

"He doesn't have to deny it. He was asleep. I had to wake him."

"And since waking him you've had another of your man-to-man talks with him?" Schmitty asked.

"I have not. There's no need for any talk. I know he didn't

do this tonight and now I see I was wrong about last night as well. He didn't do that either."

"You know who did?" Schmitty asked.

"How could I know who did? Do you think if I even had a suspicion of anyone, I'd hold back on telling you?"

The inspector shrugged. "Maybe you wouldn't," he said. "But believe me. I've had witnesses who did just that. They waited forever before telling what they knew and they just never wanted to tell it at all."

"A man who let suspicion stand against his own son when he could say the word that would stop it?"

"It's a hard choice, but I've known situations where it was made. If somebody has to take the rap, it's not as heavy on a juvenile. He'll get off easy where an adult wouldn't."

"That's the craziest insinuation," Gibbons shouted.

He was screaming again.

"It's not an insinuation, Mr. Gibbons," Schmitty told him. "Nobody is suggesting that it is what you are doing. You asked me a question about what other witnesses have done and I told you what some of them did do."

"Those weren't men. They were animals."

"In my line of work I meet a lot of animals, but let's get back to men and boys. You say he was asleep when the shot was fired. Shot didn't wake him. Screams didn't wake him. All the excitement afterward didn't wake him. You had to wake him."

"And that's the truth. I'm taking my oath on it."

"Very well. It's the truth as far as you know it. Where were you when you heard the shot?"

"Mrs. Gibbons and I were in our room asleep. The shot woke us."

"And it didn't wake the boy. It seems to have wakened everybody else but not the boy. Where does he sleep?"

"In his room. Where would he sleep?"

"This end of the house? Away from the garden?"

Gibbons shouldn't have hesitated. Even the moment of delay was transparent. He wanted to lie about it, to say that Eric did have his bedroom at the street end of the place. He almost did say it, but obviously he knew it was a lie he could never make stand up. Reluctantly he answered.

"He's a boy," Gibbons said. "When I was a boy, I slept that soundly myself. It's something you lose as you grow older. Can't you remember how well you slept when you were a boy, Inspector?"

Schmitty answered the question. He gave every evidence of subjecting it to serious thought, however, before he spoke at all. When his answer did come, it gave Tootsie Roll nothing.

"I remember," he said. "Loud noises woke me just the same as anybody else, just the same as older people. The difference was that, after being wakened, I could get back to sleep a lot faster than I can now and a lot faster than older people could."

"We're all built differently," Gibbons murmured.

"Yes, Mr. Gibbons. In some ways we are, but in some ways we are all much the same. I just want to be sure I have the picture. You tell us the boy was asleep. You weren't sitting up watching the late late show on TV or reading or anything like that while your son slept beside you. You were in your room and he was in his. When you went into his room after the shooting, you found him in bed and he appeared to be asleep. Do I have that right?"

"Not appeared to be," Gibbons insisted. "He was asleep."

"Did you watch him for any length of time before waking him?"

"Why would I do that? A shot had been fired. A woman had been killed. I had to talk to him. I never for even a moment thought of waiting."

"You had to talk to the boy and there was no time for waiting. Tell me what you had to talk to him about."

"This. What was happening. What people would be thinking. What the poor kid was going to be put through. I had to tell him I'd been wrong about the windows. I had to tell him I'd done him an injustice. I had to assure him that I was his father and that I knew the truth and I was standing back of him and that he wasn't to be afraid, no matter what anyone said or did. I was his father and he was to count on me. I wasn't going to allow this to happen. Someone had been framing him and I knew it."

Schmitty sighed. "A pity you couldn't have spared a few minutes before you woke him," he said.

"A pity I had to wake him at all, considering what I was waking him to."

"Yes," Schmitty said. "That, of course, but I was thinking something else. If you watch somebody for a little while, you sometimes can tell real sleep from pretended sleep. On one quick look there's no way you can know the real thing from the counterfeit."

"He was asleep."

"I'm not asking you to say he wasn't. We just had to be clear on your evidence for saying he was."

"He was asleep, but anyhow it doesn't matter. Even if he had been awake, he couldn't have fired that shot."

"Now that's something else," the inspector said. "What's your basis for saying that?"

"No guns. I'd taken away his guns."

"After last night's shooting? That was the way you punished him? You took away his guns?"

"Part of his punishment. I took away his air rifle and his hunting rifle. I was also taking the cost of all those broken windows out of his allowance. He was going to be a very long time paying the bill."

Lou Garcia scowled. He was just a young precinct detective and Inspector Schmidt, chief of Homicide, was doing the questioning. Schmitty caught the scowl.

"Detective Garcia has a question," he said.

"A couple of questions, sir, but one for right now on the guns."

"Right," Schmitty told him. "You'd better ask it."

"Last night," Lou said, "putting holes in windows, that was air-rifle stuff. The time before, shooting the hawk, that would have been a shotgun job. What was fired tonight was no shotgun and no air rifle. That was a hunting rifle." He turned to Gibbons. "You say you took away his guns. Then you say that after last night you took away his air rifle. Which was it? Gun or guns?"

"That's just what I mean," Tootsie Roll said. "I took away his air rifle after last night. It was the only gun he had left. I took it and locked it in the closet of my room. I was keeping it there till I would have time to dispose of it. His other guns, his shotgun and his hunting rifle, I took away from him after he shot the hawk and those two I did dispose of. They weren't in the house tonight. They haven't been since the day I learned about his killing the damn hawk."

"You disposed of the shotgun because he'd used it to kill the hawk and you were punishing him for that," Schmitty said. "What had he done with the hunting rifle that made you dispose of that as well?"

"His punishment was no more hunting. To bring that home to him the hunting rifle went with the shotgun. If he was going to be an irresponsible child, he would have to make do with the air rifle, a toy gun."

"When you say you disposed of them," Schmitty asked, "how did you dispose of them?"

"I threw them away."

"Shotguns and rifles are expensive," Schmitty remarked.

"And he had bought them with money he had saved up out of his allowance and out of gifts he'd had," Gibbons added. "He had been a long time saving for them. I wanted him to learn a lesson. I didn't sell them. I didn't want him realizing anything from them. I didn't lock them away. I wanted him to have no question in his mind that I would ever let him have them again. I thought he had to feel it as a total loss if it was to be a proper lesson."

"Where did you throw them?" Schmitty asked.

"I took him with me and I drove across the Verrazano Bridge. I made him throw them out of the car, over the side, into the harbor."

"And as soon as you had the time you were going to take another drive across the bridge with him and you were going to make him do the same thing with the air rifle?"

"Yes. After last night I thought the lesson hadn't been properly learned, but now, of course, I know better. I did the boy an injustice."

The inspector turned back to Lou Garcia.

"You had another question?" he asked.

"Yes, sir. I have."

"Go ahead. Ask it. If I'm overlooking something . . ."

"It's not that, Inspector. It's only that we were here, Mr. Bagby and me. We were here. We saw it. You weren't here."

"You didn't see anything," Gibbons snarled. "There wasn't anything to see."

"There wasn't anything to see, Detective Garcia," Inspector Schmidt purred. I've never known him to give it a more silken touch. "You tell us what you think you and Mr. Bagby saw and Mr. Gibbons will clear that up for us."

"I wanted to talk to Mr. Gibbons," Lou explained. "We tried the garden side of the house and we got no answer there. I was sure these people were up because they had lights on all over, every room in the house. We went through to the street to try at the front door. All the lights were on at this end, too, and we saw shadows on the window shades. Three people's shadows rushing around in here. It looked pretty frantic. When I rang the bell, they froze. You know, Inspector, standing perfectly still, not moving at all. Maybe if you're absolutely quiet, they'll give up and go away. Like that, Inspector. Then when I rang again, two of them went off and it was just Mr. Gibbons. He came and opened the door. That's the question, Inspector. Why lights all over? Why all the rushing around? What was the panic? Was it looking for something or was it hiding something away?"

The inspector turned to Gibbons. The question had been asked. He was waiting for an answer.

"It was Mrs. Gibbons."

The way Gibbons said it, it seemed as though he was expecting the inspector to take that answer as responsive to Lou Garcia's questions. Schmitty didn't. He gave it the analytical approach.

"Lights all over the house would seem to indicate that you had lost your wife and had been looking high and low for her," he said. "But then shadows of three people on the window shades and all three frantically rushing about, that would seem to indicate that when you found her, you were all three of you looking for a place where she could be hidden away." He tossed a significant glance in the direction of the two cupboard doors Gibbons had hurried to push shut. "I can understand your eliminating the pot cupboards to find her some more comfortable place," he added.

Gibbons caught the sarcasm. He flushed. It was an improvement. Flushed was more becoming to him than livid.

"Mrs. Gibbons," he said, "is a sensitive woman. She's nervous by temperament, high-strung. She doesn't stand up well to shocks. The shooting terrified her. She was frightened, afraid that a murderer lurked in every shadow. Lights throughout the house, that was to reassure her, to show her we were all right. There was no one here. So there's the frantic rushing about or what looked like it to your man here and to my spying neighbor. Mrs. Gibbons was feeling faint. We were rushing about trying to find something we could give her to buck her up."

Lou Garcia didn't wait for the inspector to pounce on that one. Lou was steaming.

"Something like a soothing frypan or a big stew pot she could hide her head in?" he asked.

"The boy doesn't know where we keep the brandy," Gibbons said. "So he rushed around looking in ridiculous places. His intentions were good. He wanted to help his mother."

"And the lady?" Lou was in there, pressing. "Is that the way she always faints, at the gallop?"

"Mrs. Gibbons was hysterical."

It was feeble. Hysterical and faint are not mutually exclusive. We all know that, but the kind of hysteria that produces fainting does preclude any running about. Nobody said it; but, if Gibbons couldn't read from Detective Garcia's face that Lou was thinking it, Tootsie Roll was just no good at reading faces.

Schmitty took it deadpan. He had other questions.

"Let's go back to the guns for a moment," he said. "The boy had no guns tonight. You had made him throw his shotgun and his hunting rifle into the bay and you had locked away his air rifle. So much for the boy's guns, or am I underestimating his arsenal? He never had more than the three?"

"The three," Gibbons said. "The shotgun, the hunting rifle, and the air rifle."

"Okay. Then what about you? What guns do you own, Mr. Gibbons?"

"None. I've never cared for the sport. I own no guns and I never have owned any."

"Mrs. Gibbons?"

"No."

"Then elimination of the boy's guns eliminates all guns? No firearm of any description in the house?"

"That's right. Oh, somewhere around there might be a

forgotten cap pistol or water pistol left over from when Eric was little, and, while we're on the subject, I had better amend my statement about any guns I may have owned. I did have cap pistols and water pistols when I was a little boy and I haven't any idea of what may have become of them, but they disappeared long before I was grown and even longer before we moved into this apartment. They've never been here."

If you are under questioning and you want to register your contempt for the questions being asked, I know of no better way to do it than by just such overmeticulous prolixity.

"We won't worry about those," Schmitty told him.

It isn't that the inspector doesn't recognize sarcasm when he is confronted with it. He never allows it to ruffle him.

"It's good to have something eliminated," Gibbons said.

He seemed to think he was accomplishing something by taking the lofty line.

When the inspector suggested that it might be useful if he could ask young Eric a few questions, the suggestion did nothing toward bringing Tootsie Roll down to earth.

"That," he said, "I shall not permit. I will speak for the boy."

"It may be necessary that we have his answers and that we have them directly from him," Schmitty said.

"I'll have the advice of my attorney on that," Gibbons snapped. "Meanwhile the answer is no."

Schmitty shrugged. "It can wait," he said. "By the way, where is the boy now?"

"He took his mother to her room. She was going to lie down and he was going to stay with her. I would hope by now she's been able to get back to sleep and that Eric has gone to his own bed and he is also asleep."

Schmitty looked at his watch.

"That's right, Mr. Gibbons," he murmured. "We are keeping you up, aren't we? I can't think of anything more now, certainly nothing that won't keep until tomorrow. I want to thank you for your time and patience."

Gibbons met that with no more than a curt nod. He was losing no time about leading us toward his door. It was obvious that he couldn't be rid of us too soon.

Since he must have realized that the inspector would most likely at this point be heading for the Hobbes house, the natural way to have taken us might have been through his place to the french doors that would let us out into the garden. It may only have been that he was in no mood for extending us any courtesies he could deny us, or it may have been that he didn't want us going beyond his kitchen, where he had kept us penned up throughout the questioning.

We were out of the place and Gibbons was in the act of shutting his door behind us when the inspector turned to leave with him something he would not enjoy thinking about.

"I have to check in with the precinct people," Schmitty said, "and get myself updated on how things stand, but I do think we'll have to trouble you with a search of your apartment."

"You'll need a warrant for that," Gibbons snapped.

Schmitty sighed. "I'd hoped it wouldn't be necessary," he said. "You see, Mr. Gibbons, I'm sure all of you who live in these houses would be relieved if we found that some stranger had gotten in and done the shooting. You'd like that, wouldn't you, Mr. Gibbons? Your boy cleared and without the guilt falling on any of your friends and neighbors. Since I understand there's no way out of the garden except through one of these houses to the street, we can't ignore the possibility that the killer might still be found hidden somewhere in one of the houses."

"Just hanging about, waiting for you to find him?"

Gibbons was piling the sarcasm on.

"Having been unable to get out before the police cordoned the area off," Schmitty said. "If he's still here and we
could find him, it would simplify things for us and be of the
greatest benefit to you. It's not only your boy you have to be
thinking about, Mr. Gibbons, but your frail and nervous
lady. If there's a killer hiding somewhere in one of the
houses, even if he doesn't kill again, you should consider the
effect on your wife's nerves. If I lived here, I'd want to be
very sure of the safety of my house."

If in putting it that way the inspector had been having
any expectation of softening Tootsie Roll up, I could see no
indications of success. I sensed, if anything, a hardening of
the man's suspicion and hostility. I can't say that I saw him
putting his guard up since, after all, he'd had it up from the
first; but he did seem like a man who had been standing
armed against a frontal assault and who now felt a need for
marshaling further defenses to protect his flank.

I tried to help. "I should think," I said, "that all our
houses should be searched. I, for one, wouldn't care to go
back into my place tonight unless the police went through it
first and I could be certain that I wouldn't be walking in on
a killer who might be hiding away in there."

"You," Tootsie Roll bleated, "are not in my position."

The man was inviting me to mind my own business.

"As long as there's a chance that you have a killer holed
up in one of your houses," Schmitty said, "you're all in the
same danger."

Gibbons hesitated. The inspector had him hung up on the
horns of a dilemma. He could hardly deny this possibility of
danger without sticking himself with the assumption that
the killer was one of our own little group, an assumption he
had every reason for knocking down since among ourselves
it was his Eric who was the prime suspect. On the other
hand, it was evident that he was not only opposed to any
police exploration of his premises. He dreaded the possi-

bility. Our penetration, even though it had been only as far as his kitchen, had had him in a quivering sweat.

He surrendered, but only grudgingly, and, even at that, he laid down conditions.

"All right," he said, "if you must, but only if you've done every other house and apartment first and then only if the invasion of my privacy is limited to looking for some stranger holed up in here. There will be no questioning of either my wife or my son and there will be no poking into places too small for a man to hide in."

The inspector made no promises and we pulled away from there. Tootsie Roll left it at that. He made no effort to exact a promise. He had been too long eager to lock his door after us. Nothing could have induced him to delay further the happy moment.

Out in the street Inspector Schmidt turned to me for advice.

"You know your neighbors," Schmitty said. "If we do you first, will it soothe them down on the invasion-of-privacy bit? Nobody's immune, not even my old friend George Bagby. That's one way they can take it, but there's also the other way. Are they going to think I'm playing favorites? Bagby's my old friend I see first to Bagby's safety and meanwhile the women and children can be murdered in their beds. You know them. Which way are they likely to swing on this?"

On character reading alone, I had no way of knowing. We were, as you may have noticed by now, a mixed lot. On almost anything it could be expected that our reactions would be at least as varied as were our individual characters. For my answer to Schmitty I fell back on the one thing about which I expected the group would be unanimous.

"Since," I said, "they are all of the opinion that any shots fired around here can be fired by no one but the Gibbons kid—some of them will hesitate about saying as much and particularly to you, but they are all thinking it—with that in mind, none of them is likely to be much worried about unknown killers lurking under beds. So if you do my place first, you'll be showing them that you're not playing favorites."

Schmitty grinned. "Good thinking," he said. "I'll tell them we're going to have to search and we'll see how they take it, but that probably will be best, doing your place first."

It was one of those minor decisions, seeming to make no great difference either way. If anything, at that time it could have been rated as nothing more than making a public-relations choice, but we'd hardly finished kicking it around before it changed.

Since Gibbons had not invited us to go through his ground floor to reach the garden, it was left for us to return the way Lou Garcia and I had come, by way of my place. I unlocked the door and came face to face with my landlord. Mike Grassi was on the stairs. It seemed to me that he must have been on his way down to go out to the street, but I told myself that I could be wrong. He might have been on his way up and had turned on the stairs when he heard my key in the lock behind him. He stood halfway up the stairway. Planted that way with his hands clasped behind his back, he looked down at us.

"Inspector Schmidt," he said.

"Mr. Grassi," Schmitty responded.

They knew each other, having met a couple of times of an afternoon when Schmitty had been with me and Mike dropped down for one of those waiting-for-the-shower-to-be-free drinks we sometimes had.

"I bet this is something you never expected," Mike said. He seemed to be babbling. "That it would be us over here getting you out of bed this time of night."

"Everything gets me out of bed," Schmitty said. "We're just going in to search Baggy's place."

He gave Mike the rundown on the thinking. A killer from outside who might not have made his getaway before the police had us cordoned off and who would still be hiding in one of our houses.

"We've had shooting before and it wasn't anybody from outside," Mike said.

His words astonished me. When last I'd seen him, he'd been aching with pity for Gibbons. Now he wasn't yelling Eric but he seemed to be at least on the edge of doing it.

"That's been the assumption," Schmitty said. "Not proven. Not enough to stop us from making sure by following through on all routine."

"Nobody up in my place," Mike said.

"How can you be certain?"

All this time that Mike was arguing with the inspector he was mounting the stairs, taking them slowly a step at a time, walking up backward. It's true that he was talking or listening all through, but it would have seemed more natural if he'd stayed put on the step where we'd surprised him or else had come down a few steps to talk with us. Even if he was in a hurry to be upstairs with his wife and boys, I'd have expected that he would have been going up the stairs in the more ordinary fashion, pausing now and again and turning his head to speak. Backing up the stairs the way he was looked most peculiar. He wasn't, after all, withdrawing from the presence of royalty. Inspector Schmidt commands no such protocol.

"If there was anybody, and I'm sure there isn't," Mike said, "he'd hide some place where the people had emptied out. Like George's place. George has been out and busy ever since it happened and a lot of the other neighbors the same thing. I went out but I didn't let the wife or kids come.

They've been upstairs right on through and I've been back up there. Nobody there."

"Better to be sure," Schmitty told him. "Look. Suppose we come up and do you first. That way you'll have us out of your hair and you can go back to bed."

Mike had reached the top step by then. He planted himself there.

"No way, Inspector," he said. "Not now, not later. The kids were up and roaring. My wife has only just got them settled down. Now she's taken a tranquilizer and is trying to get to sleep. They're going to be left alone."

"If they are alone," Schmitty said.

"I'll check," Mike promised. "I'll look in all the closets. I'll look under all the beds. I'll look any place else you'd like to suggest, and if I find him I'll turn him over to you. I promise you that."

"And if you get shot?" Schmitty asked.

"We'll let the insurance company worry about that," Mike said, forcing a laugh. Meanwhile he backed away from the top of the steps and retreated out of sight. His voice came down to us even when we could no longer see him. "Anybody comes up here tonight," he said, "I'm going to throw him down the stairs. I swear to God I will. I don't care who it is. You, Inspector. George. The whole damn police force. Anybody, and I mean it."

After that speech we heard him shut his apartment door and I heard his key turn in the lock. I tried to think if I'd ever heard that before. I was certain I hadn't. We keep the street door locked, of course, but I'd never locked the door from my apartment to the hall I share with the Grassis and they had never locked the door from their apartment to the hall at the top of the stairs. I wasn't ready to say that in all the houses around the garden the people had been as easy one with the other as I had been with the Grassis, but it was

my guess that we were far from being alone in this practice
of locking doors against the outside world but not against an
upstairs or downstairs neighbor.

I whistled softly. Schmitty echoed my whistle.

"There's one buddy of yours who has the jumps tonight,"
he said.

I led the way into my place, turning on lights ahead of us
as we went through. It's Bagby's response to the energy crisis. I never leave a room these days without switching off
the light behind me. Even if I'm in a great rush, even when
my mind is on something else, it's become a reflex. I don't
even know I'm doing it.

I was still thinking about how I could explain Mike Grassi
to the inspector, trying in fact to explain him to myself,
when I came to the door of my living room, the one that had
at its far end the garden door.

I flipped on the living-room lights and I stopped in my
tracks. It was so sudden a stop that it had Schmitty and Lou
Garcia just about climbing up my back. They weren't much
behind me in seeing what I was seeing. The inspector
shoved me to one side and, with Lou at his heels, he
charged past me and headed into the room.

It was right there in plain sight. On its garden side that
living room has a wall that is virtually all glass. There is the
glass-paned door to the garden and alongside it a strip of
windows with a long windowseat set below them. It was
under the windowseat just as it might have been if it had
been hastily pushed all the way back where in the shadow
of the windowseat it might have been less arrestingly visible or even out of sight. It lay in a position where it was
only just under.

It was a rifle and it wasn't anybody's pop gun. It was a
hunting rifle, quite enough for bringing down a moose, easily enough for bringing down a woman.

I made a quick recovery from my paralysis of astonishment. By the time the inspector was ready to pick the weapon up for closer examination, I was at his side. He sniffed at the barrel and held it so I could have a sniff. The powder smell was unmistakable.

"This," said Inspector Schmidt, "should make you feel like you're the Verrazano Bridge."

V

During the time we had been occupied with Gibbons the police contingent on the scene had grown. The technical men were now on the job along with the precinct detectives. Schmitty had them take over on the rifle and he detailed the precinct boys to do the search for that possible stranger in hiding and, not incidentally, for any firearms they might turn up. He set it up for them to do all our places with the exceptions of the Gibbons establishment and of Mike Grassi's place. The assumption was that we had already been through those two places and Schmitty let the assumption stand. No purpose could have been served by suggesting to any of the others that they might prefer to make the inspector wait till he could obtain search warrants.

None of the other neighbors was setting up any opposition to the search. It may have been that thinking that two of our number had already submitted to it made the others prone to welcome it, or it may have been just as easy without. I had no way of knowing.

For the inspector the next order of business was to have been crossing over to Daphne's house for an inspection of Jill's body and of the Hobbes premises as well as for an interview with Daphne Hobbes. Our coming on the gun postponed that for a little. It brought me to the top of the interview list.

Schmitty questioned me and, since Lou Garcia had passed through my living room with me when we had gone out to the street to hit the Gibbons' doorbell, he also questioned Lou.

There was no need for him to check on whether it was my rifle. He knows me better than that. I own no guns. Way back at the beginning of my association with the inspector he had given me a revolver. It had seemed a good idea. Following him around on one of his cases, I could never know when I might find myself in a situation where the going would be so rough that I would be the better for being armed.

I carried the thing only until the first time we did come on such a situation. I drew and I fired. My aim was so wildly erratic that Inspector Schmidt had a change of mind. He told me there could never be any situation in which I wouldn't be better unarmed. I had to agree with him and I happily returned the revolver.

So that made two questions the inspector could consider had answered themselves. It was not my gun and I was not the one who had fired the shot that took Jill Armitage's life. It wasn't that such unquestioning acceptance of my innocence in any way amounted to showing me special favor. The air-rifle performance the night before had been the work of a marksman. The rifle shot that had drilled Jill cleanly through the head had been a work of similarly expert marksmanship. All that expertise eliminated me. Bagby was too inept.

This freshly fired rifle which could be presumed to be the murder weapon had, nevertheless, turned up in my living room. Questions of when it had come there and how had to be considered. There, however, neither Lou nor I could be of any help to the inspector.

The door alongside that windowseat had not been locked at any time. When on first hearing the shot and screams I had rushed out across the garden, I had left the door standing ajar behind me. Going in and out after that, when I went in to call the inspector, when I came through with Lou Garcia, I never bothered to shut the door. When Lou had moved to do it, I'd told him not to bother.

On going through with Lou I had hit the light switch just inside the garden door to light the room for our crossing of it, and on habit, as we left the room by the door opposite, I had flipped the light switch there to darken the room behind us. Neither Lou nor I could say that the rifle had not been there under the windowseat when we had passed through the room because we had gone straight through without looking at anything and that space under the windowseat had not at any point in our passage been in our line of sight. The rifle might have been there then and it might not. We had no way of knowing.

"That leaves earlier," Schmitty told me. "You heard the shot. You heard the lady scream. You went rushing over to the house across the way. You came through here and all the way across the room you were faced directly in the right direction for seeing the rifle if it was there then. You didn't see it?"

"No, Schmitty, I didn't."

"After you'd been over there you phoned me. Where did you phone? From here?"

"Yes, from here."

"And you didn't see it then?"

"No."

"Can we figure that it was put there later, maybe before you came back this way with Detective Garcia, or maybe while we were next door watching Mr. Gibbons sweat? What I'm asking is, can you say for sure that you would have seen it if it had been there?"

I had to think for a moment before I answered that one. The inspector gave me the time. He didn't hurry me. I thought about it and, when I did answer, I was certain.

"No better than when I came through with Lou," I said.

"Maybe it was there and maybe it wasn't. If it was there, I didn't see it."

"When you came in the same way just now," Schmitty reminded me, "it jumped at you. How could you have missed it before?"

"When I came through the first time, after the shot and the screams," I explained, "I was moving in the direction to see it but I was alone. That's why I took the time to think and try to remember before I answered you on just how. I know the room. I know where the furniture stands and all that. Coming through alone, I didn't bother with lights. I'm certain of that. I dashed across and out to the garden and I did it in the dark."

Lou was looking bothered. The inspector noticed it.

"You have a question, Garcia?" he asked.

Lou shook his head. "I don't know," he muttered. "Mr. Bagby may only be thinking he remembers."

Obviously worried that it might be sounding as though he doubted my word, he hurried on to explain. Coming through the apartment with me, he had seen me go through my routine of switching lights on as we came into each room and flipping them off as we left each room. He sensed that it was one of those acts that habit has made automatic. It was something I did without thinking, without making any conscious decision. He was wondering whether a man mightn't have acted from habit without having the first trace of memory of having performed the automatic act.

"I see what you mean," I said, "and you could be right. I think not, though, because this business of flipping lights on and off isn't quite as automatic as it seems. Coming through with you and again with you and the inspector, I did do it and it was automatic, but automatic acts don't just happen. There has to be something to trigger them and the trigger here is having someone with me. I can find my way around here in the dark. I can't expect that you or Inspector Schmidt could do it. Automatically I lit the room up for you. When I was alone, I came through in the dark."

"You really remember you did?" Schmitty asked. "Or do you think you remember this time because a lot of the time it is what you do?"

"I remember," I insisted. "If anyone asked me, I'd say I know this room. I know it so well that I could do it blind-folded. You think you can but it's likely to be not quite that good. Going through in the dark, I misjudged my distances by a bit and I stubbed my toe against that table leg. I wouldn't have done that if I'd given myself any light."

Schmitty inspected the table I indicated. It's one of those small, light jobs. It stands at the arm of the sofa where it's handy for holding an ashtray and for setting down a glass. He satisfied himself that in crossing the room as I had, it would have taken only a couple of inches of straying off the most direct route to bring me afoul of the corner of the table. He did better than that. He observed that the table had been knocked just a little awry. Instead of standing parallel to the arm of the sofa, it was slightly at an angle with one of its corners poked into the upholstery of the sofa arm.

"Okay," he said. "Now what about when you were in here to telephone?"

"I remember that," I told him. "I picked up the phone and, since I'd come back in and again hadn't turned on the lights, I couldn't see to dial. I switched on the table light by the phone to dial and I switched it off while I was talk-ing to you. Don't ask me why. I didn't want anybody out in the garden to see me phoning."

The inspector was satisfied. "So it's anytime after the shot was fired," he said. "Nothing we can eliminate except the few minutes you were in here, telephoning or coming through one time and another. Anything going on here in those few minutes you might have known, but for all of the rest of the time it's wide open unless we come up with another witness who can shut any part of it off for us."

"Sorry not to be more help," I said.

The inspector shrugged. "Another inconvenience of the energy crisis," he said. "Another little score to settle with the oil producers."

We went across to Daphne's house. The technicians had taken over her drawing room and Mrs. Hobbes had moved or had been moved upstairs. We could see her up there through the windows of her upstairs sitting room. From the look of it she might have been holding court. I could see some of the neighbors and a couple of precinct detectives. There was the silver coffee service and Daphne was presiding over the coffeepot. She was pouring. There also seemed to be drinks going. It could well have been another of Daphne's parties.

I did try to put the thought aside as unworthy but I couldn't rid myself of it. She had thrown a party on the occasion of the slaughtered hawk, why wouldn't there be another for a slaughtered shrew?

I must admit I was torn between one curiosity and another. I didn't know which was pulling me the more, the impulse to go upstairs and join the company in Daphne's sitting room or the wish to stay with the inspector to be on top of the evidence as he collected it. Once we were in the house, however, it became evident that Schmitty expected me to stand by with him. That settled it. The wake or whatever it was upstairs would have to wait. I did think some about the neighbors I had spotted through the windows. This time, so far as I could see, Daphne had about her more of the women than the men. Gus Weller was up there with his wife. The Wellers had the house next door to Daphne's. Otherwise it seemed to be wives without husbands and only one unattached male. That was Jack Jackson. He was up there, but no Gibbons and no Grassi.

Nobody would have expected it of Lollypop or Tootsie Roll, but the Grassis worried me. They were good neighbors. It just didn't seem like the Clara Grassi I knew to have gone back to sleep instead of crossing the garden to do what she could toward pulling Daphne out of shock and getting her back to sleep. But then there had been Mike on the stairs. He had been nothing like the Mike Grassi I knew.

The body had not yet been moved. Ordinarily it would have been out of there before this, but the word had come through to the precinct men that Inspector Schmidt was on hand and the body had been left till the inspector could see it. He appreciated that. He appeared to be finding the body interesting and the surrounding scene even more absorbing.

She lay as she had fallen, and from the position of the body and the relative position of objects on the bar the inspector reconstructed precisely where and how she had been standing when the bullet hit her.

The bottle from which she'd been pouring had, of course, dropped from her hand with what had been its contents poured out on the floor in a wide pool. On the bar, however, there was a smaller pool of spilled whiskey. That was just alongside the partly filled glass that still stood on the bar.

She had been pouring the liquor into the glass she'd had standing on the bar. There had been that split second between the slug hitting her and the bottle dropping from her hand as she toppled to the floor, and during that fraction of a moment the pouring liquor had missed the glass and made that little pool on the bar. Schmitty measured the dead woman's height. Moving to the window, he matched that measurement against the height of the bullet hole in the glass that had only that afternoon been installed. The two measurements were so identical as would make no difference.

"Level shot," he said. "No shooting down at her from above."

Coming back to the bar, he stationed himself where Jill had been standing to pour herself the drink she was never to enjoy. Sighting on the bullet hole from there, he looked across to the houses opposite. I tried it from behind the bar, putting myself in line with the inspector and with the bullet hole.

Need I tell you what else I saw along that same line?

It wasn't the door to my place but it didn't miss my door by much It was the foot of the spiral staircase that gave the Grassis their access to the garden. Since that staircase comes down right beside my door, I had to feel grateful that Inspector Schmidt, chief of Homicide, knew me as well as he did. My quick second thought was to wish that Schmitty had known Mike Grassi equally well, but the thought was immediately followed by a wave of doubt. I couldn't put from my mind the absurdity of Mike's performance on the stairs and I had to wonder whether I knew my landlord as well as I'd thought I did.

When we moved on upstairs, I was expecting that the inspector would do a quick job of clearing the neighbors out of there so he could have Daphne Hobbes alone. From what I knew of the lady I could have told him that things would have gone better for him without the large audience in attendance. With all those people about her, Daphne would inevitably be performing more in the role of the hostess than as a witness, and her social manner would be the last thing Schmitty might need from her.

I didn't bother to say anything because it never occurred to me that there would be any need. To go in for any partying in the course of working an investigation had never been Inspector Schmidt's way, but this was my night for revisions in what I thought I knew about people. First it had been Mike Grassi. Now it was the inspector.

If Mrs. Hobbes welcomed him as yet another guest at her impromptu gathering, he was not going to take any official tone with her. He just went along. He even seemed to enjoy it. It could be that it was the manner of her welcome that did it, for Daphne Hobbes, at least, confronted me with no astonishments. She ran true to form. The moment we appeared in her sitting-room doorway she was off and winging.

"George," she said. "I knew you'd come. I knew you wouldn't desert me and you've brought your clever friend. How sweet! Do hurry and introduce us. I've been dying to meet him. It began the first time I saw him through your windows across the garden and that's been ever so long ago. I told myself then. There was a man I just had to know. If you'd been more observant, George, you would have seen long before this that I was drooling with desire."

I introduced the inspector.

"Lovely, oh, lovely," Daphne chortled. "Now you delicious man," she said, turning her joy full blast on Schmitty, "I want you to be as comfortable and as homely with me as you are with George."

This had to be a new experience for Schmitty. He had been called a wide variety of things in his time, but never before "a delicious man." He took it with admirable aplomb and responded only to the "homely."

"No problem about being homely," he said. "It's the only face I've got."

Daphne looked contrite. She came near to overdoing it. Only a little more and she would have been abject. That would never have suited her style.

"Oh, fiddle," she moaned. "I am the bloody fool. I do try to speak properly. I work hard on perfecting my American and then I slip into the most obvious gaffes. When you say homely, you mean plain. For homely you say 'at home.' I know that. How could I have forgotten? You aren't homely at all. You're a fine figure of a man and I like your face. Intelligence. Character. It's an admirable face."

A lesser man than Inspector Schmidt would have been squirming under that, but Schmitty took it in stride. He played along.

"A man has to have something to go on the front of his head," he told her. "It does."

"Then you do understand you will be at home," Daphne persisted, permitting more than a trace of imperiousness to creep into her tone. "I want you out of your boots and into a drink immediately." She stopped short and waved both her hands back and forth in the air in front of her face as though she was trying to erase the words she had just spoken. "I'm not doing at all well with my talking American tonight," she explained. "I had one Americanism I was determined not to use, not here, not now. I've been telling myself that I couldn't say 'name your poison.' That would be bloody right inappropriate to the occasion, but being so careful of that, I've slipped right back into being excruciatingly English. You don't call them boots over here, not unless they go on up your legs. So, please, Inspector, do take off your shoes. I know you want to, and why ever not, especially since I have?"

She thrust one foot forward, kicking the hem of her negligee out of the way to put her naked toes on display. Grinning, Schmitty sat down beside her and shucked out of his shoes.

I knew what that was doing for him. It goes back to his rookie cop days. That was in the old times when a patrolman walked a beat. He didn't ride around in a squad car. Schmitty insists that his feet never recovered from those days of beat pounding, but he is, nevertheless, without envy for the lads in the squad cars who can do their patrolling sitting down. He predicts that they will find themselves going through the rest of their lives with uncomfortably tender behinds.

Having seen to the inspector's ease, Daphne urged drinks on the both of us. Schmitty asked for coffee. I poured myself a shamefully prodigal splash of Daphne's magnificent cognac. She gave me a dazzling smile of approval.

"You'd do well to imitate George," she told the inspector. "The moon is over the yardarm. We've looked."

"Give me a raincheck," Schmitty said. "I am on duty." He looked down at his socks and wiggled his toes. "Even if I don't look it," he added.

"I'll hold you to that, Inspector," Daphne said, pouring his coffee. "You will come back and take proper drink with me just as soon as this is over."

"It's a promise," Schmitty said.

His mention of duty opened the door. Sylvia Weller grabbed the opportunity.

"Those poor, poor parents," she moaned, "and that poor, unfortunate, crazy boy. How are they taking it, Inspector? Is there something we could do for them? After all, the mother . . ."

"What boy?" Schmitty asked. "What mother?"

His questions got nowhere. They were overridden by his hostess. She went into a great flurry of remembering her manners and nothing could go forward until she had done the rounds of the whole company. She did the introductions with full regard for all the niceties. Schmitty was presented to Sylvia Weller. He was presented to the other ladies. Sylvia's husband and Jackson were introduced to Inspector Schmidt.

Jack Jackson was the last to be introduced and, even as the inspector was turning from him to return to Sylvia Weller, Jackson pushed in with his opinion.

"That's what's wrong with us in this country," he growled. "That damn kid is a cold-blooded killer and we're supposed to bleed for him. We're supposed to lay him gently on the couch so some shrink can go into court and tell the jury what was wrong in the murdering sonofa's toilet training that made him like he is. Nobody's got to bleed for the kid and not for the parents either. If it was up to me to do it, I'd string the both of them up along with their precious son and not because they did something wrong when they were getting him housebroken. Because of what they did yesterday, or I guess it's because of what they didn't do."

"What could they do?" Sylvia took up the argument. "That child is insane, hopelessly, totally insane, and none of us realized it until this happened tonight. If none of us realized it, how would they? They're his mother and father. When it's your own blood, your own child, you can't help deceiving yourself. You can't believe that your boy could be a horror."

I knew the Wellers. A childless couple, they had never had any children. Maybe it was because Gus was always leaving too much in other women's beds to have anything left over for his wife, and maybe it was because Sylvia had never been in a position to allow herself pregnancy's nine-month relaxation from total preoccupation with the preservation of her looks, the looks she felt she had to have if she was to remain at all attractive to Gus Weller even if the most she could hope for was her position as perennial also-ran.

The childlessness, however, may not have made any difference. Is there a woman anywhere, whether she's been a mother or not, who is not convinced that she has some sort of inside track on knowing how a mother feels? And maybe they do know. Who am I to say? I'm not a woman.

I don't even set myself up as being an authority on how men feel about things. Some of the time I know how I feel, but I never let myself forget that each of us is different. Watching Gus Weller while his wife was having the argument with our vigilante-minded neighbor, Jackson, I was wondering whether Gus could be the cold fish he appeared to be. The best I could make of it was that there were so many women in his philandering life that one more or less was of no consequence. So Jill Armitage was dead. Too bad, but nothing to break up over. He'd already had her. He had already moved on to someone else, and there would be still others to look forward to in his future. Jill left no gap.

I was wondering about Sylvia too. It could have been a lot of other women I know, and I would have assumed that they had been reading books and were subscribing to the argument that calls all killings "acts of madness" and that contends that anybody who performs an act of madness is, by definition, mad. I'm not suggesting that Sylvia Weller might not also have been reading those books, but I did have to recognize the possibility that she was impelled to take the most generous possible attitude toward Eric Gibbons and his parents since the boy had, after all, done her the service of eliminating a rival or, if you will, a former rival.

Poor woman, she must have known that the elimination of one wasn't likely to be any more good to her than just that, the elimination of one. It was going to change nothing for her. There would always be another and another ad infinitum, but, nevertheless, relief from one pain is relief. We take it and we allow ourselves to luxuriate in it. We don't destroy it by reaching out to take on tomorrow's pain prematurely.

With my mind running along on these lines I was only half listening to the answer Jackson was pushing at her. It contained nothing unexpected. I could follow it with half a mind.

She could call the killing crazy if she liked but he preferred another adjective. He called it vicious. His argument, however, was that what any one of us chose to call it was beside the point. The job done with the air rifle on Daphne's windows the night before might not have been enough to tell anyone that the boy was crazy or he was vicious or anything like that. It was more than enough to tell the dullest idiot going that here was a boy who was not to be trusted with guns.

"To leave any kind of a weapon around where that kid could lay his hands on it," he insisted, "was criminal. Okay. His old man worries about burglars. He keeps a weapon in the house. You know, a pistol or a revolver, whatever it was. He feels he has to have it handy for the protection of his wife and his baby boy. But damnit. First things first. You've had it shown to you that your baby boy is a crazy fool with guns. You get rid of it, and quick, even it it does mean you'll be letting the burglars and the bogeymen come flooding in."

Sylvia sniffed. "Monday-morning quarterbacking," she said. "We can all be wise after the fact."

"I was saying it yesterday," Jackson boasted. "After what he did with the air rifle, that kid's father should have busted both the boy's arms. That would have put his shooting off, a couple of broken arms. He should have been my kid."

"I hope you never have one," Sylvia snapped. "I've never heard anything so savage."

They had argued themselves into a dead end. There was nothing more for either of them to say. Sylvia just glared at Jackson and Jackson's smirk couldn't have been more self-satisfied. It was evident that he liked being called a savage. I could imagine that he saw himself that way, the noble savage perhaps.

Inspector Schmidt waited just long enough to make certain that the flow had come to an end and that by speaking he wouldn't be cutting off anything more that might be coming at him spontaneously. Nothing more came. There was a lull while Daphne poured more coffee and people had their other drinks freshened.

The inspector moved in on it. "I'm a stranger here," he

said. "Fill me in. Who are we talking about? The way I've got it, there are two families over opposite that have children and boys in both families."

I said nothing since I was aware that Schmitty knew the answer to this question he was asking. Since he obviously wanted to hear it from someone else, it was more than obvious that the someone else wouldn't be his friend, George Bagby.

The others all hung back from making the direct accusation. They had all been going along without the first question of where the guilt fell, but nobody relished taking on the role of being the informer. It may seem that for Jack Jackson this was a sudden change of heart; but, when I looked at him in the expectation that he would be the one to speak, I could see that nothing had changed. He was lying back and watching us with his self-satisfied smile that was almost a sneer. He was sitting back to test us, waiting for us to prove that we were a bunch of sentimental slobs.

It was Daphne Hobbes who answered Schmitty, but only by indirection.

"The little Italian lads," she said. "Oh, not those little charmers. Never in all this world. The babies are Correggio cherubs and, as they grow, they grow handsomer. They are loves, all of them."

"That leaves the folks that have just the one boy?" Schmitty asked.

"A thoroughbred," Jackson said, giving up on the rest of us. "By Tootsie Roll out of Lollypop."

Of course, Schmitty would have needed to have that explained, but I took care of it later. At that moment we were interrupted. Daphne's young relative arrived, the man I knew from seeing him across the garden. I've mentioned the elegant formality of the times they would sit down to dinner for two. On this occasion the young man had those dinners topped. He must have come straight from a most formal party. It was white tie and tails, the total elegance from the gleam of patent-leather pumps to the glow of the impeccable opera hat.

Although Daphne had been beaming and twinkling, she had in the course of the argument between Sylvia Weller and Jack Jackson dimmed down considerably. Now, at sight of the young man, she came right up to a bright glow of delight.

"Gordon," she shouted. "What a lovely surprise! And to think you would bother to come and let me see how beautiful you look. And you do, my sweet. You're a dazzler. You're a stunner. Absolutely smashing."

The dazzler took a bow and made it complete with self-mocking flourishes.

"The truth of it, Daph," he said, "is I've come to see how beautiful you look or even to see if you were looking well at all. Not to be too fancy about it, darling, I came to see if you were all right."

"You will have been drinking champagne," Daphne said. "There won't be any cold. Do you mind putting brandy down on top of bubbly? Your uncle did it all the time."

"I don't have to tell you that my uncle was a better man than I ever hope to be. I'll rest on what I've already taken aboard."

"Prudent, of course, my darling," Daphne beamed. "But also a touch stuffy. Surely you're much too young for prudence."

"And a little too old for folly, Daph, my dear."

Daphne shuddered. "A chilling thought," she said. "Coffee, then?"

"By all means, coffee."

In the course of pouring his coffee, Daphne introduced the young man to the assembled company. He was Gordon Hobbes, her late husband's grandnephew.

"Possibly I should be precise," she said, "and call him my

nephew-in-law. It's a delicious law since it makes this charmer my nephew."

Gordon Hobbes was playing along with her, keeping the occasion comfortably frothy, but only to the point where her introductions reached Inspector Schmidt. Her mention of Schmitty's title did it. The young man sobered. It was obvious that no matter how energetically his aunt might be exercising her social graces, there could be no avoiding the fact that she was confronted with a law that even she could hardly call delicious.

Quickly he apologized to the inspector.

"I'm interrupting," he said. "I am sorry."

Graciousness can be catching.

"No harm done," Schmitty said. He turned back to Jackson. "You were giving me the blood lines," he said. "Your thoroughbred has a name?"

Jackson scowled. "Don't go handing him to me. I want no part of him. The name is Gibbons, Eric Gibbons."

"Lives right across the garden, next door to Bagby?"

"Next door to Bagby, apartment under mine."

"Which one's Eric, the son or the old man?"

"Not the old man," Jackson said. "The old man's Tootsie Roll."

I was holding no brief for any of the Gibbons clan, but this did seem an unnecessarily nasty performance. I found myself liking our new resident less all the time, but I was keeping out of it. If at any point Schmitty might want to shut Jackson up, he would know how to do it. Since it was clearly Schmitty's choice to keep the flow coming, it was not my place to intrude my distaste.

The one who did break in was Gus Weller.

"Come on," he growled. "So they have those icky names for each other. It's no crime."

Daphne sighed. "I suppose it isn't," she said. "So many

things that needn't be crimes are that one would think that anything that tiresome and saccharine would be."

Sylvia Weller returned to the battle. "The boy is insane, Inspector," she said. "You'll have to do something about him, for everybody's safety and for his own."

As she finished speaking, she turned to Jackson. Tacitly she was asking him how he liked them apples.

Jackson sneered. "What Mrs. Weller is trying to tell you, Inspector," he said, "is that the law had better put a protective arm around that dear little, sweet little, murdering pup before some horrid savage like me gets his hands on the son-of-a-lollypop."

"We've just been talking to the boy's father," Schmitty said. "He tells us that his son was asleep. He slept right through. Young, you know. A good, sound sleeper. Shot, hubbub, nothing wakes him. His father had to get him up."

It would seem as though that should have touched off an explosion from my vigilant neighbor, but he took it with no more than a resigned shrug. The explosion came from Sylvia Weller.

"And you believe that?" she asked.

It was more than a question. It was a shriek of outrage.

"Right now," Schmitty told her, "I am doing nothing more than collecting facts and listening to statements. Sorting out what I can and cannot believe comes later."

"And innocent until proven guilty," Gordon Hobbes added, throwing in nothing but words.

It could have been irony or a simple statement of principle. He was just presenting the thought and leaving it to be taken whichever way any of us might choose to take it.

"Always that," Schmitty agreed. "Couldn't say it better myself."

Having drawn Schmitty's attention, Gordon Hobbes seized his opportunity.

"I don't want to gum anything up or cause any difficulties," he said, "but if it's all right with you, Inspector, I should like to take my aunt out of here. Not tomorrow or sometime later or anything like that. I want to do it right now. Let's say just as quickly as she can put her shoes on. If you are going to be needing her at any time, for any reason, you have my promise that you will have immediate access to her, but I am convinced, Inspector, that for her safety she should be losing no time about getting out of here and, more than that, nobody should know where I'm taking her."

From almost the beginning of that it was impossible not to see that Daphne was at war with herself. Torn between her natural imperiousness and her delight with young Gordon's concern for her, she remained silent far longer than I would ever have expected of her, but imperiousness finally won out. It couldn't have been otherwise.

"You are sweet, Gordon," she said, "but you are also talking nonsense. This dreadful thing has happened, but it has happened. It is done now. It is over with. It's ridiculous to think it will just go on and on or that it would be permitted to go on and on. Inspector Schmidt is here. The house is densely populated with his lovely police officers. My boy, you are being absurd and, I'm afraid, even something less than polite in even suggesting that they would permit me to come to any harm."

Gordon Hobbes was prepared for that. After all, he did know the lady he was dealing with.

"Call me a worrier if you like," he said, "but you are going to let me have my way in this, just for my peace of mind. I know full well that the inspector and his men would spare nothing in keeping you safe, but they have other things to do as well. I expect the inspector will welcome my taking that part of what needs to be done off his hands. I can give full time to just the one thing, protecting you, and that is what I shall be doing until Inspector Schmidt has eliminated the danger, as I know he will."

"Of course he will," Daphne countered. "He will take that unfortunate lad into custody and that will be the end of it, all dangers eliminated."

"And if it should be something less simple?" her nephew asked.

"Oh, fiddle! What's to complicate it?"

"Your friend is dead, Daph, murdered. She was killed by mistake. Can we expect that her killer will be satisfied with that? Any old killing? One is as good as another? I think not. I think he will try again and I'm not prepared to go on any assumption that he will go on making mistakes."

Daphne said nothing. She just stared at him. There was nothing in her expression that could indicate that he had convinced her. It was just that he had her confused and bewildered. I cannot say he didn't have me wondering as well, and I wasn't alone. We all looked at him, speculating on what he could know that we didn't know.

"Not the Gibbons boy?" somebody asked.

I don't remember exactly who did put the question. It was one of the several women who were there. They had rushed to Daphne's side and had stayed on, partaking of her cognac and liqueurs and coffee.

"Somebody who'll go on and on shooting women around here?"

That was another of the women. They had all turned frightened faces toward the broad windows that looked down on the garden.

Gus Weller laughed. "One after another like ducks in a row," he chortled, "until he gets the range on the right duck."

"That's not funny," his wife screamed at him.

"I wish it could be funny," Gordon Hobbes continued.

"He's made one mistake and I don't have to tell you, Daph, that I don't want him trying again and getting it right the second time. What I do have to tell you, though, since you seem not to have thought of it, is that we don't want him, not you, not I, trying again and making another mistake either. It's your neighbors' safety as well as your own."

Inspector Schmidt had been listening and saying nothing. Now Daphne Hobbes was turning to him, obviously expecting that he would line up on her side and demolish her nephew's argument for her. Schmitty responded but not with argument. He had questions.

"You think the shot that killed that woman downstairs was meant for your aunt?" he asked.

"I think it's dangerous to assume otherwise."

"What makes you think that?"

"Call it a feeling I have."

"What do you know about what happened here?"

"What I heard on my car radio."

"And that was?"

"That a woman had been shot at this address, and, of course, I knew the address. That panicked me, but then they said it wasn't Daph. It was a guest. That was a relief, but not much. When they went on and said the dead woman had been wearing some robe thing of Daph's, that clinched it for me. I knew I had to get her away from here and fast. I knew I had to get her out of sight."

Daphne broke in on him, but now there was nothing of imperiousness in it. I had never thought I would see this redoubtable lady with a glistening of tears in her eyes or that I would hear any tremulousness in her voice.

"Dear boy," she murmured, and her voice was so low that it was only because of her habit of precise enunciation that her words were understandable. "The moment you came in, you went right there to where you're standing and ever since you haven't moved from that spot. You put yourself

there between me and the windows and you have been
screening me from the windows with your body. Your young
life, lad? My almost-finished years? Better you than me?"

"Nothing like that, Daph, my darling. He doesn't want
me. I'm safe as churches wherever I stand."

VI

I've always liked the thought that among my neighbors I'm valued for myself alone, but I couldn't kid myself. To some extent, at least, I had always been basking in Inspector Schmidt's reflected glory. You know how that goes. I wasn't just George Bagby. I was the man who knew the inspector.

It was a strange feeling, therefore, when all of that changed. Suddenly my connection with Schmitty was gaining me nothing. Frustration, resentment, anger, all the hostile feelings of my neighbors began rubbing off on me. Any thought my neighbors might have had that there could be a special advantage in having me around wiped away. Who needed Bagby and that inspector of his? Why didn't they just get lost?

There were, of course, some exceptions. First of all there was Daphne Hobbes, but I suppose she didn't count since her nephew, Gordon, had snatched her out of our garden group. She was feeling anything but unprotected. Similarly, the Gibbons three didn't count. Their position was even more special. When I come right down to it, the only true exceptions were the Grassis.

They had been my friends and nothing was changing that. It never entered their minds to blame me for the way Inspector Schmidt was performing and, if at any time they might have been at one with the other neighbors in dissatisfaction with Schmitty's procedure, they were too kind to let me have any indication of such feeling. Much less would they have had any thought of blaming me for what the inspector was doing or not doing.

The trouble was that there wasn't a one among the residents—and in that number I have to include myself and even Eric Gibbons' ma and pa—who wasn't dead certain that in the murder of Jill Armitage the inspector was confronted with the most open-and-shut of open-and-shut cases. One could concede, it seemed to all of us, that for building a case that could be taken into court he might have to do some measure of sleuthing; but, as we saw it, anything of that sort would follow after the main event. The main event, of course, would be the immediate removal from our midst and into custody of Jill Armitage's killer.

Why didn't the inspector do the obvious thing? Why didn't he at the outset put the arm on Eric Gibbons and leave his questioning and his looking around for a more suitable time; that is, after the menace had been removed? Since I myself didn't understand the way Schmitty was going about this thing, I could hardly expect that my neighbors would understand.

The difference between me and them, however, was that I had been through situations like this with the inspector too many times before, times when his procedure seemed to be flying in the face of all good sense, and, when on coming down to the wire, I discovered that instead of having been sucked in by appearances as I had been, Inspector Schmidt had been taking a more penetrating look and had been assessing appearances against the logic of events.

In short, just on his track record, I had long since reached the place where in the face of the way a thing might seem to me, I would always be ready to say, "The inspector knows best." My neighbors hadn't been at his elbow down through the years, watching him establish that track record. They just couldn't believe he knew what he was doing.

Since what he was doing seemed to be going on the as-

sumption that Eric Gibbons was no more suspect than any
of the rest of us, it was the consensus of the garden group
that Inspector Schmidt was exhibiting an outrageously cava-
lier disregard for our safety.

Jack Jackson was loud and long in yelling law and order
and in calling the inspector a bleeding heart. Equally, however, the Wellers and particularly Sylvia, who in Jackson's
estimation had exhibited some bleeding-heart proclivities of
her own, were hardly reticent in their criticism of Inspector
Schmidt. Whether the individual attitude toward Eric Gibbons was punitive or pitying made no difference. Eric
should have been taken into custody without delay—for our
good, for his own good, for every conceivable reason.

It wasn't that the inspector was doing nothing; but whatever he did do was rated for nothing since he hadn't put
Eric Gibbons under arrest.

What he did first didn't seem too much off the mark. He
cooperated with Gordon Hobbes in persuading Daphne to
indulge her nephew in the young man's wishes. He expe-
dited her removal and he provided a police escort for Gordon's Jaguar. Only Gordon Hobbes, however, and expect-
edly since it was his idea, seemed to think the removal
properly took precedence over arresting Eric, but it was uni-
versally expected that the arrest would at least be the next
move.

When it was not, when instead Schmitty wandered
around checking on the progress his men were making with
the searches he had set up for all our houses around the garden, the grumbling began. The impatience flared up into
anger, and Jackson came up with a brilliant idea.

Since Inspector Schmidt was clearly incompetent, somebody ought to go into the Gibbons place and make a citi-
zen's arrest. I half expected he might even try it, but he
didn't. It could have been that there were just too many
police around, but I was more inclined to think that friend

Jackson was all noise and no guts. This was, after all, consistent with the way he had been from the first. He talked tough, but he did nothing.

How long the inspector might have gone on checking on those searches I don't know. He was called away from them by another interruption, another Daphne Hobbes nephew. This one, however, was no in-law. He was blood kin. One could have known him for that on sight. He was a masculine version of Daphne as she might have been some thirty years before. I was guessing him to be in his late forties or possibly just turned fifty. Apart from these discrepancies of age and sex, there was only one visible difference between nephew and aunt. I couldn't believe that Daphne would ever have looked so soft.

His name was Roderick Pagnell. He was no night owl. He would never have known of this dreadful thing before he had seen his morning paper if it hadn't been for an insomniac friend who, on having heard the radio report, rang him up to wake him with the news of the lurid doings in the house of his only living relative.

Whether blood kin or in-law, Daphne's nephews seemed to be running to type. Roderick's first thought had been identical with Gordon's. Aunt Daph had to be scooped out of her house and removed immediately to a secret and safe place. He had jumped into his clothes and hurried over bent on doing precisely that.

When told that the lady had already been removed, he looked as though he didn't know whether to be relieved or even more alarmed. He wanted to know where she had gone. He insisted on knowing. It was imperative that he go to her at once and make certain that proper provisions had been made for her safety.

The officers working in the Hobbes house could, of course, tell him nothing. They had to buck him on to the inspector. By that time he was exploding with outrage. Outrage appeared to be epidemic around our garden that night.

He was the only person Daphne Hobbes had in this world and he had a right to know where she had gone. Was she alone? She must not be alone. Someone had to be with her at all times. That was essential.

"She isn't alone," Schmitty told him. "Her nephew is taking care of her."

"I'm her nephew," Pagnell bleated.

It was the anguished yelp a king might emit if told that a usurper had sneaked in under his crown.

"Nephew-in-law," Schmitty amended. "Gordon Hobbes."

The words hit Pagnell like a kick in the groin. He turned white. He gasped. He spluttered. In a moment he shifted from looking as though he were about to faint to looking as though he were about to foam at the mouth. He didn't wait for full recovery from what to all appearances had been an all-but-lethal shock. As soon as he had pulled himself together enough to manage articulate sounds, he gasped his question:

"Where has he taken her?"

Schmitty tried to persuade him that his aunt was in good hands, that she was being well looked after, afforded every sort of protection.

"Part of her protection is that nobody knows where she is," he explained. "That was agreed between Mr. Hobbes and me."

"I'll bet it was," Pagnell snarled. "And I'll bet it was his idea."

"We agreed it would be best that way."

They were having this exchange out in the garden, just off the door to my place. Schmitty turned away from Pagnell and started into my living room. Pagnell grabbed at his shoulder and tried to spin him around. A man would have to be a fool to try it. Schmitty isn't the biggest guy I've ever known and he isn't the strongest, but he's nobody you can push around. Even without knowing him, just on the look of the man, his weight, the solid way he's built, the way he carries himself always in balance, you can see he's nobody's toy top. This guy just doesn't spin.

Without even turning around, the inspector took a hold on Pagnell's wrist and handed the man's paw back to him.

"Try to behave yourself, Mr. Pagnell," he said. "I'm not walking away from you. I'm just going to phone Hobbes and tell him you're here and you're worried and you want to help. We'll see what he says."

"He's not shutting me out. Tell him that."

"We'll see what he says. You can talk to him yourself."

"He's nobody. I'm of her blood. You shouldn't have let him take her off this way. You should have waited for me."

Schmitty didn't bother with that. He went on in and picked up my phone. Pagnell tagged after him, just about walking on the inspector's heels. I was about to follow them but at a more decent distance, but at that moment Mike Grassi popped up beside me. For all I knew he had come from nowhere.

"Give me a minute, George," he whispered.

I stopped with him. When a friend is gray-faced and sweating, you don't deny him anything as small as a minute, but I was letting him have only one ear. The other was cocked to pick up whatever might be going at the phone. Schmitty dialed. Pagnell was trying to see the numbers the inspector was spinning but Schmitty was having none of that. Keeping Pagnell blocked off, he put enough arm motion into his dialing to make the process do double work. He elbowed Pagnell off his back.

Meanwhile Mike was at my ear.

"Have they found the gun?" he was asking.

I tried to give him a quick answer. I didn't want to miss anything.

"They found a gun," I said. "A rifle, recently fired and chucked in here under my windowseat."

"Then it's the gun," Mike said.

I could have told him that in all probability it was the gun, but the real answer was waiting till they would have the bullet out of Jill and the ballistics boys had made the comparison with a test bullet fired out of the rifle we'd found in my living room. I didn't stop for it. I saw no need to be that technical with Mike and in any case I didn't have my mind on it. I was more interested in Pagnell and in Inspector Schmidt and in the telephone.

Schmitty got through and it was obvious that he was talking to Gordon Hobbes.

"I have a man here who says he's another nephew," he was saying. "Has Mrs. Hobbes got another nephew?"

"Rick?" he asked, after a pause for listening. "What's that, Rick for Richard?"

Pagnell made a grab for the phone but Schmitty shouldered him away from it.

"Rick for Roderick," Schmitty said. "That's right. Roderick Pagnell. That fits. It's the name he gave me. He wants to talk to you."

Pagnell reached for the phone. It was evident that he expected that the time had come when with no more ado the inspector would hand it over to him. Schmitty almost did, but abruptly he changed his mind and hung on to it. It appeared that the nephew-in-law had something more to say to the inspector before he would be ready to take on the nephew.

"What does he look like?" Schmitty said, evidently echoing a question that had come to him over the phone. "Spitting image of your aunt except that he's fiftyish, I'd say, and he isn't a woman. Can you picture a man made of Silly Putty or something soft like that?"

Evidently Gordon Hobbes got the picture and it matched

up with the man he knew. The inspector handed the phone over to Pagnell.

"Hobbes wants to talk to you," he said.

Pagnell snatched the phone out of Schmitty's hand.

"Thanks for nothing," he muttered.

Schmitty shrugged and came over to where I was standing.

"Hobbes wants him," he said. "He even seems to think the guy can help. Every man to his own ideas."

"It gets him out of your hair," I said.

"Nothing," Schmitty reminded me, "gets anybody out of my hair until we have this thing cleared up."

He said it without bitterness. It was a simple statement of fact and I had the feeling that he was thinking it was something I should have known.

Mike was right alongside me. As far as I had been able to see, my answer about the rifle had satisfied him, but now he seemed to be wanting something more. I turned to him, but this time it was Inspector Schmidt whom Mike wanted.

"Inspector," he said, "could you give me a couple of minutes? There's something I've got to tell you. I've been a damn fool."

"You think I need to know that?" Schmitty asked him. "Or have you got something more on your mind?"

"I'd like to tell you," Mike said.

"Right away," Schmitty promised. "As soon as I've gotten our friend Rick out of here."

Pagnell came away from the phone.

"I'm going right over there," he told Schmitty. "Gordon says you have a policeman with them. Thank you."

"For nothing," Schmitty said.

It wasn't an Englishing of the Spanish *por nada*. The inspector was just adding for him the words which this time around Pagnell was leaving unsaid. Pagnell didn't stop to pick it up. He scuttled off. I had a feeling that being wanted might have been a new experience for him. He wasn't going to miss any of it.

The inspector turned to me.

"Ever seen that one before?" he asked.

"No," I said, "and even on short acquaintance I can guess why I haven't."

"Make your guess or do I have to pull it out of you?"

"You said the other nephew wants him," I explained, "and obviously he's been invited to go over and join the guard. It's my guess that Aunt Daphne is going to be less than overjoyed. She's a tough bird and she likes people that have some steel in them. She won't tolerate people who bore her and soft people disgust her. It's my guess that he hasn't been around because she wouldn't have welcomed his coming and she also wouldn't have been shy about telling him as much."

"The other one—the in-law—he had been around?"

"Comes to dinner at least once a week and he house-sits for her when she goes away."

Mike Grassi stepped into it and backed up my guess.

"George is right about her," he said. "She does like her people tough. Jill Armitage, for instance. She took to Jill right off and that's all the Armitage dame ever had to offer, toughness and a sharp tongue."

"Don't forget her fair white body," I said.

For a moment Mike looked as though he might be about to go into a *de-mortuis-nil-nisi-bonum* routine, but he evidently remembered that when you're talking about the dead to Inspector Schmidt, nothing but the good is not going to be good enough. If Schmitty is to do his job, he's going to have to know all of it.

"She never let anybody forget that," Mike said, "at least nobody who had balls, but that didn't mean anything to the old lady. She's the wrong sex."

I wasn't forgetting that Mike had wanted a word with the

inspector and it took no clairvoyance to know that it couldn't have been any of these words. Now, however, he was behaving as though he had forgotten all about it.

I knew it wasn't that. Poor Mike was in a state where he would have liked not to remember. I could tell that there was something he had to do and, even though he was too much man to let himself put off the doing, he was enough fallibly human to grab at this postponement that was not of his own making.

That the inspector was also not forgetting may be taken for granted. Since I hadn't missed noticing Mike's agony, you can be sure that Mike's symptoms hadn't escaped Schmitty's attention. You may think the inspector was setting up this diversion to give Mike some time for pulling himself together, but I knew better than that.

Inspector Schmidt is not an unkind man, but he is a pro and on the job he's all pro. He's not without pity, but I've never known him to allow pity to come between him and anything he feels needs doing. What he was now doing I had watched him do many times with other people in similar situations.

Somebody comes to him all set to volunteer information. It is information the volunteer would much rather not have to give. The man is going through hell, braced to tear the words out of himself, and for the inspector's purposes that's what's wrong with it. The man is braced. He has prepared the words he is about to use and the inspector is suspicious of prepared words. There is too strong a likelihood that they won't be all the words there are. Something might be held back.

This is technique. You give your man a breather, suck him into even some small measure of inattention. Then by pulling a fast switch back to the main event, you give him no time to pull his prepared words back together and he just might blurt out something he had been planning not to say.

TWO IN THE BUSH

If you look back over this little talk we were having, you will see that it was Schmitty who started it. He asked me the question. At the first moment when it looked as though Schmitty and I had come to the end of that, however, Mike stepped into it and kept it going. Now he moved to open yet another door on it.

"And Big-Noise Jackson," Mike said. "Him, too. Mrs. Hobbes took to him from the first she met him. Maybe when she gets to know him better, she'll see through him and realize that he's not so tough. He's just a blowhard. His talk is all hard-guy but there's nothing back of the talk."

And it was then that the inspector made the switch.

"You had something you wanted to tell me," he said.

He caught Mike with his mouth open. Mike closed it and swallowed hard.

"I'm a dope," he said. He stopped short. You could almost see the thoughts as they were scurrying around inside his head, trying to reassemble in what had been Mike's prepared line. His pause drew out and, with the inspector's gaze never leaving him, he had to break it. In a panic rush he plunged ahead. "I didn't want you searching my place," he said. "I didn't want it because I have a rifle upstairs. That's why I didn't want any searching."

"You have a rifle," Schmitty told him, "and your first idea was you'd get rid of it and say nothing."

Mike gulped. "No," he said. "Not that way. I didn't chuck the gun in here under the windowseat. Mine's still upstairs. I want to hand it over to you."

If Mike had been hoping that Inspector Schmidt might take that as an act of simple good citizenship, even though a bit delayed, Schmitty was quick to straighten him around.

"You want to hand it over to me," he said, "because you find you're stuck with it. You were going to take it out of the house and dump it somewhere, but when you got as far as the street door, you saw that was no good. We've got the street cordoned off. So then you had to take it back upstairs to hide it away till the cops would be gone and you could take it out and dump it."

"I said I was a dope," Mike mumbled.

"And you thought I was another," Schmitty growled. "You had bad luck. We came in and caught you in the hall just when you were going back up with the rifle. Did you think I didn't notice that you were going up the stairs backward with your hands behind your back? Or maybe you expected me to believe you were going up that way because it's good for your skiing muscles? I know a guy, he shacks up with somebody who lives on the fifth floor of a walk-up down in the Village. Every time he goes to her he walks up the five flights backward because it's good for his skiing muscles. I don't know whether you ski or not, Grassi, my friend, but I watched you back up those stairs and I knew you didn't have skiing on your mind."

"I was stupid," Mike said. "I don't pretend I wasn't. I'm sorry. I'm apologizing. I want to turn the damn gun over to you."

"Now that you've had time to clean and oil it?" Schmitty asked.

"If it's cleaned and oiled, it's because that's the way it was when I got it. I've never had it out of the wrappings it came in."

Schmitty pounced on that. "A new gun," he said. "You buy yourself a rifle and right off a woman in the house opposite gets shot."

I was wishing he'd lay off. It wasn't as though he was still looking for the weapon. Granted that he was still waiting for ballistics to come up with the solid evidence on it, but it could hardly have been that he thought there was any chance they wouldn't.

I knew what he was doing and ordinarily I would have been with him all the way. The inspector has never been inclined to go easy on people who try to withhold information even if they think better of it and come through with it in repentance before he's come around to wringing it out of them. That is as it should be. I've never had any doubt of that, but Mike Grassi was my friend. I couldn't enjoy watching him sweat.

"It's not a new gun," Mike said. "I've had it fifteen years and more."

"And never out of the wrapper? Come on, Grassi."

"I can explain."

"It better be good."

"If you'll just let me."

"Go ahead. I'm listening."

He could explain and it was a good story. It answered all the questions and it even carried its own built-in corroboration. Mike was no marksman. He hated guns and he wanted no part of them. The rifle had belonged to his older brother and even from the little Mike said of him, that older brother had been as different from Mike as a brother could be. Deer hunting had been a passion with him and this rifle had been his most highly prized possession. For all the difference between them, however, they had been close.

I can imagine it. Mike's that kind of a guy. He's warm in all his relationships, but family ties for him are passionately close.

"Al," Mike said. "Al was my brother. He was killed a little more than fifteen years ago. At night over on the Jersey Turnpike. One of those heavy fog patches you drive into over there sometimes. Al was maybe driving too fast, but so were a lot of other guys. It was a twelve-car chain smashup. Only eight of the drivers came out of it alive and some other people who'd been riding as passengers. Al didn't."

So all of brother Al's stuff had come to Mike. There had been just the two of them in a large family of sisters. Mike had had no use for the gun as a gun. It never meant anything to him except that it had been Al's and it had been the thing that Al had loved above all other possessions.

"I had no use for it," Mike said, "but it had been his and he had set such store by it. I couldn't make myself sell it or give it away or throw it out or anything. It's been like a part of Al, a part of him I still had. Even though all this time I never touched it or even looked at it, it was there in my closet. I had it. I go into the closet for shoes or slacks or something and I see the package. I think of Al."

You get the picture? Here's a man who owns a rifle and whose ignorance of guns is total. He knows them so little that he could think that a gun that hadn't been used in more than fifteen years could ever be mistaken for a gun that had been freshly fired. Only a man who was that ignorant about firearms could even have had the thought that he had to get rid of that rifle. Furthermore, a man who was that innocent of any knowledge of guns would have to be even more innocent of any skill at marksmanship.

"I'll have to see the rifle," Schmitty said.

"I'll bring it down."

"No," Schmitty said. "We'll go up with you."

On the stairs he relented a little, although he was still rubbing in on Mike what Mike had done.

"Not backward this time," he said. "I guess you don't ski."

"Matter of fact, I do. I'm crazy about it, but maybe not that crazy. I never heard about going upstairs backward."

"If after tonight your skiing's improved," Schmitty said, "let me know."

"I'm hoping that after tonight maybe it'll be my brain that's improved," Mike told him.

We didn't have to disturb Clara or the kids. Mike's closet opened on the hall outside their bedroom door. Clara had the closets that were in the bedroom itself and she was asleep behind the closed bedroom door. The kids slept in rooms at the other end of the hall and in rooms all over the next floor up.

Mike pulled his closet door open and indicated the long, narrow package. It was a paper-wrapped box. The inspector picked it up and the three of us trooped downstairs with it. The paper wrapping had gone dry and brittle. Under Schmitty's grip it split.

"Let me open this on your kitchen table," Schmitty said. "I don't want to get in bad with Mrs. Grassi for scattering dry paper crumbs all over her rugs."

"She picks up after me and nine boys," Mike said. "Think she'd notice picking up after one more?"

He led the way to the kitchen, nevertheless, and snapped on the light. Schmitty started untying the cord but, like the paper, it was dried and brittle. It broke at his touch. As soon as he started on the paper wrapping, it split at every fold. All through this process Mike was watching and moment by moment he was getting redder in the face.

Watching that package come undone, he could hardly have had the smallest fear of anyone doubting his story. The dry and brittle cord and the untouchably frangible paper were all the evidence anyone could ever have wanted to prove that this rifle had not been out of its box that night.

Unwrapped and lifted out of the box, the weapon offered its own evidence. This was a good rifle brother Al had owned and he had given it loving care. It was clean and it had been carefully oiled and wiped, but oil that had been coating a surface for fifteen years and more does show its age. The rifle would need to have been cleaned of its old oil before it could have been fired.

Schmitty returned it to the box.

"You'll need fresh paper and string," he said, handing Mike the box.

Mike didn't take it from him.

"I'm turning it in," he said. "It's yours. Do with it whatever you do with guns people turn in."

"You don't have to do that," Schmitty told him. "You can put it back in the closet."

Mike shook his head.

"No," he insisted. "Now that I've had to come to think it out, I can remember Al without it. I don't want it around. There are the boys. If any of them or all of them grow up to be like Al in every other way, I'll like that, but I don't want them wanting to shoot anything. I'd rather they didn't enjoy killing things. I'd be grateful if you did take it away."

VII

It was a great day for collecting weapons. There was the rifle that had been dumped in my living room and now there was Mike Grassi's heirloom. The additional ones were harder to come by because for them there was a lawyer in the act and he went through no few of the motions for protecting his client. Since he was a good lawyer, he didn't go through all of them. He persuaded his client to waive some of his rights and, even though it was obvious that the course he had pressured his client into taking was skillfully designed to put the best face possible on the unfortunate position his client had put himself into before he got around to seeking legal advice, this good attorney was offering more expediting than obstruction. The inspector isn't wont to refuse any expediting that might come his way.

Gibbons could have held out for a duly executed search warrant and that would have taken time, but with police all around the house time could have done Gibbons little good. There would have been nothing he could do with it beyond sitting embattled in his castle and waiting for the inevitable blow to fall. He couldn't get away. He couldn't get Eric away, and he, no more than Mike Grassi, could get any guns out of the house.

Yes, there were guns and on his lawyer's advice he was ready to hand them over instead of waiting for them to be found. When we came downstairs from Mike's place, one of Schmitty's men was waiting for us. It was Tim Clancy and you'd have to know Tim to appreciate what follows. You'll

never find a man who looks more like an Irish cop than Tim
Clancy, not this side of Hollywood. Aside from his name
and his looks, however, there's nothing about Tim that fits
the cliché image. You'd have to know him, though, before
you could recognize that. Just on his looks, anyone would
jump to conclusions.

"We've got an attorney, Inspector, and he wants to see
you at your earliest convenience," Tim told Schmitty. "And
you'd better hope you're not allergic to shamrocks."

"Who's he representing?"

"Man next door, Gibbons."

"Did you get the Harp's name?" Schmitty asked.

He and Tim have their private jokes.

"Brennan, and with a brogue so thick you can float an an-
vil on it."

"That," said Schmitty, "will have to be Patrick Joseph
Brennan, the flannel-mouthed mouthpiece."

"Have to be," Tim agreed. "There can't be two the like of
him."

"The brogue," Schmitty said, "turns on and off. For me he
turns it off. Talking to Officer Clancy, he turns it on. If you
want to catch the full blast of it, you should hear him sometime when he's before a jury and he's managed to get even
one Irishman on it. Where is he?"

"Next door with his client. He said to call him the first
minute you'll be free."

"Okay, call him. I'll be in here."

The inspector indicated my place.

Patrick Joseph Brennan came over, and he came armed
not with his brogue, to be sure, but with weapons. In one
hand he carried an air rifle. In the other he had the real
thing, a hunting rifle. Tucked under his arm there was a
shotgun.

"My client, Inspector, is surrendering these to you."

"A little late," Schmitty commented, "or did he need the time to go diving and bring them up out of the bay?"

"He waited only as long as was necessary if he was to proceed with advice of counsel."

"He consulted you," Schmitty said, "and since it was your judgment that he hadn't a prayer of smuggling them out of the house and disposing of them by driving across the Verrazano Bridge and dumping them in the water, you advised him that he would look better if he volunteered them before we secured a warrant and went in and found them."

"I advised my client to surrender them. I object to your imputing motives for my giving my client this advice."

"Objection noted," Schmitty said. "We'll strike out Inspector Schmidt's imputation."

"Clients without experience or legal knowledge almost invariably do something foolish when they try to cope without waiting for the advice of counsel."

"Like lying to the police, or didn't he tell you?"

"He told me. He wasn't under oath, Inspector."

"And he gained ample time for cleaning and oiling this rifle," Schmitty added.

He was inspecting the weapons. Like the rifle we had just seen upstairs, these also had been given skillful and loving care. Here, however, the care was recent. Whether in the last few hours or the last few days, of course, there was no determining.

"I can assure you my client has been otherwise occupied."

"Where had he been keeping these?" Schmitty asked.

"They are the boy's. They were in the boy's room."

"You know about the earlier shootings?"

"The bird and the windows? My client has told me everything."

"Then he didn't take the guns away from the kid even temporarily?"

"No, he didn't."

"Hardly a prudent man, would you say?"

"He took other measures he thought would be as effective, Inspector."

"Such as?"

"Taking away the boy's ammunition. Unloaded guns and no ammunition available, certainly harmless."

"Not if the boy had pocket money and could buy ammo," Schmitty said.

Brennan smiled. "No ammunition and no pocket money," he said. "That was the boy's punishment for shooting the hawk. His father stopped his allowance. He thought the punishment would be more effective if he left Eric in possession of the now-useless guns, that the sight of them would rub the punishment in."

"And it never occurred to him that the boy might find a way to get money to buy ammo? What's the story on that? Where did he get it?"

"He didn't."

"Oh, come on, Mr. Brennan!"

"I'd like to explain my client's thinking and also to tell you what happened."

"I'm sure you'd like to. Do you think you can?"

Brennan grinned.

"Let me try," he said.

The inspector listened and the attorney provided an exhibition of his skill as an advocate. He touched all bases. He could well understand the assumptions Inspector Schmidt had been making. In the inspector's place he would have made the same assumptions.

"Up to a point," he said, "even Mr. Gibbons made those same assumptions, but only up to a point. When he became aware of the window-shooting episode, he assumed, as you did, that the precautions he had taken had been inadequate. In some way or other Eric had come into possession of ammunition for the air rifle. He charged the boy with it and

Eric denied it. I believe he told you that he took no stock in the boy's denials."

"He blames himself for that," Schmitty interjected. "A lot more comfortable than blaming himself for a woman's death."

Brennan chose to ignore the interruption.

"All day yesterday he was working on the boy," he said, "trying to wring a confession out of Eric. He had to know how the boy could have laid his hands on the ammo. It seemed to him that the performance with the windows, bad as that was, would be nothing to what he feared Eric might have done to procure the ammunition."

"Like stealing?"

"Breaking windows is naughty," Brennan said. "Stealing is criminal."

"So is murder," Schmitty reminded him.

"Ah, but we haven't come to that."

Brennan was in there with his own reminder.

"Okay, I'll wait till you catch up."

"Eric could not be moved. He had no ammunition. He hadn't gotten any ammunition. He hadn't shot at the windows. It was someone else who had done it, someone who figured to get away with it because Eric would be blamed. I understand there is a family of boys next door to them. It would be right upstairs here."

"Nine of them," Schmitty said, "armed with nothing but baseball bats, except the little ones—they have rattles."

"Not even water pistols," I added.

"For all Eric's denials," Brennan continued, "his father couldn't believe him. Since he had already stopped the boy's allowance and had already made the arrangements to send him to military school, he searched his mind for further punishment."

"Like seeing how good his pants would stay up when he took his belt off to lay it on Eric?" Schmitty asked.

Brennan sighed.

"I can't believe he wasn't tempted," he said, "but not everything is possible, Inspector. Eric is a big boy, big and strong, taller than his father, heavier than his father, and awesomely well-muscled."

"So the old man couldn't think of anything to do?"

"He thought of something. He was going to take all the guns, load them in his car, make the boy go with him, drive out to the middle of the Verrazano Bridge, and make the boy throw his beloved guns into the bay. That was on his agenda for today."

"And when he talked to me he felt that the thought was as good as the act? All it needed was a little predating?"

Brennan shrugged.

"I can understand, Inspector," he said, "how you would be thinking of a father's natural inability to conceive of his son as a murderer. Let me tell you this. I'm not the boy's father and I can't conceive of him as a murderer. But then, I must concede, I am the boy's attorney and, more than that, I've known him since the day he was born. I used to dandle him on my knee. Later I lay on the floor with him and played with his electric trains. More recently during the deer season I've taken him hunting. I've had to recognize that my own view of the boy could be a prejudiced one, and for that reason, if no other, I've been seeking out more solid evidence than my feeling about Eric."

"And you found some?"

"That I did, Inspector. That I did."

"Giving it to me or saving it for the jury?"

Brennan laughed.

"Since we won't be going to a jury, Inspector," he said, "I have to give it to you. I don't want to leave it to go to waste."

"I like solid evidence," Schmitty said.

"And so do I. It was early yesterday morning when Mr.

Gibbons came home from a trip and became aware of the window-shooting episode. It was still some hours before any stores were open, any place at all where the boy could have bought or stolen rifle ammunition. From that hour until bedtime last night, Eric was never out of the house. For whatever short time his father wasn't working on him, Mrs. Gibbons was, all through the day and the evening."

Schmitty made short work of that solid evidence.

"So for the one day mom and pop are alibiing their one and only child," he said. "He had no chance to go out and pick up ammo all that day. I'm sorry, Mr. Brennan. It doesn't knock me over."

"His mother. His father. The servants. Also the neighbors. Those were stormy sessions and they were nonstop. Shouting and wailing that disturbed the neighbors."

Schmitty looked at me. I nodded.

"You heard them?" Schmitty asked. "You heard the boy?"

"Couldn't get away from it," I said. "By noon it drove me out of the house."

Brennan pounced on that.

"See," he said. "There's a witness for the whole morning. I've already talked to their neighbors on the other side. It drove the woman nuts all afternoon. She did her marketing in the morning, but then she had a bridge luncheon and they could hardly play all afternoon for the yelling and the howling next door and the kid screaming over and over again that he didn't and he didn't. It went on into the evening when at about ten o'clock her husband couldn't take it anymore. He picked up the phone and told them that if they didn't shut it down he was going to call the police."

"Okay," Schmitty conceded. "You've got your one day. It isn't enough."

"I'd say it is," Brennan argued. "Even if we say Eric could have borrowed money from some other kid and, dead set on shooting out those windows across the way, bought ammo for the air rifle. If you like, let's even say he stole it. That would need to have been before the day we have covered, since it was the night before that that the window job was done. With me so far?"

"With you."

"All right. The boy is in a rage against this Mrs. Hobbes because she raised the fuss about the bird he shot. He has this childish notion of getting back at her by shooting out her windows. Is it reasonable to believe that he plans on taking his revenge in stages? He'll shoot at windows one night and take a rifle shot at the woman the next night? Even if you can believe he could be so stupid that when he shot at the windows and was punished for that, he would follow it immediately by shooting the woman the next night, you can't imagine him thinking he would get the ammo to shoot at the windows and, since he would undoubtedly be punished for that, he would have even a larger score to settle with the lady, and that in preparation for such vengeance he would lay in the ammunition he might need for shooting her."

"If he had a chance to buy any ammo at all," the inspector said, "I can easily imagine him getting himself all he could, ammo for all his guns. It would be just to have it. It wouldn't have to be that he foresaw the specific use he would put it to."

"Is a jury ever going to believe that? Can you really believe it?"

"My job, Mr. Brennan, has taught me to believe things that until they've happened are unbelievable. Then they do happen and I have no choice. I have to believe them. That anybody would one night shoot a hole in every window he can aim at in the house opposite and then the next night shoot one hole in one woman in that same house I would say was unbelievable. But now it has happened. I have to believe it."

"That it was done, Inspector," Brennan argued, "but not that it was Eric's doing. Eric is labeled. He's the young fool who shoots things around here. Any shooting done in this area will automatically be blamed on the boy. To make sure, shoot at the windows. That will get everybody fixed in the necessary grooved thinking. Isn't that typically a boy's prank? The spotlight is fastened on Eric. Then the next night the shooting. Who will look to anybody but Eric Gibbons?"

"I will," Schmitty said, "but not so far as to take my eye off Eric. I want to backtrack a bit. The boy's father took all the ammunition away and just left the kid the unloaded, ammoless firearms. What did he do with the ammo? Did he throw that in the bay?"

"No, he locked it in his closet and, after the window thing night before last, he locked the guns in there, too."

"And after the shooting last night he and his wife and the kid ran all over the house looking for a better place to hide the guns and the ammunition, all sorts of great places like kitchen cupboards."

"What grounds do you have for saying that?"

"We interrupted them while they were in the process, or maybe I've made the wrong guess. Maybe they were looking high and low for another rifle, the one that had just been fired, the murder weapon."

"Nonsense. There is no other rifle."

"Nonsense," Schmitty echoed Brennan. "There is another one and we have it."

"Certainly that puts Eric in the clear," Brennan said.

"Not so fast," Schmitty told him. "Not till we've had the report from ballistics. Of course, if this rifle you've turned over should prove to be the one that fired the shot that killed Mrs. Armitage, things will be simple. If not, the possibility still remains that Eric Gibbons had two hunting rifles. That's not a bad ploy, you know, to surrender one gun and say, 'See? There's my gun and you have proof right there that I didn't do it.' Meanwhile he's disposed of the other gun."

"Where? When?"

"Immediately after the shot was fired. The shot woke everybody, everybody but Eric. Why didn't it wake him? Because he's a sound sleeper or because he hadn't been asleep? He had been awake to fire the shot and, while everybody else was climbing out of bed, he was up and around to dispose of the rifle."

"Where?"

"Where we found it." Schmitty was not ready to give any more than that. "You've turned over the guns," he added. "What about the ammo?"

"What about it?"

"Where is it now?"

"Locked in Mr. Gibbons' closet."

"I'll have to see it."

He not only saw it. He took it away with him and, with it, for what they were worth, he also took away the sworn statements of Gibbons father and Gibbons son that the ammo boxes were exactly as they had been on the day of Daphne's hawk wingding when the elder Gibbons had stormed back from those festivities to confiscate the ammunition and lock it away in his closet. He had taken from the boy every last shell Eric owned. Every last shell the boxes had then contained was still there. They swore to that. Pop swore that he had counted them before he locked them away. Eric swore that he always knew just how much ammunition he had and that the quantity now in the boxes was the quantity his father had taken from him.

They also swore that the activity we had interrupted the night before had been exactly what Schmitty had suggested in one of his alternatives. It had been an hysterical search for some better hiding place for the guns and the ammo, but

not, of course, because any Gibbons had for even one moment entertained the thought that Eric might have been
guilty of Jill Armitage's killing, only because it had been obvious to them that the young innocent had been framed for
the murder.

The inspector tried them on the other alternative, that
there had been another rifle and that, not knowing that Eric
had already rid himself of that one by pushing it under my
windowseat, Tootsie Roll and Lollypop had been frantically
searching for it. Questions along that line elicited nothing
but screaming denials.

Lollypop at this junction astonished me by showing more
steel than did her menfolk. When we left them, father and
son were still shouting their less-than-coherent protestations
of innocence. Lolly, however, simmered down the minute
the questioning stopped and, when we pulled out of there,
she came along after us.

She tugged at the inspector's sleeve.

"I don't want to accuse anybody," she said.

"But . . . ?"

Schmitty knows this preamble. He was waiting for the accusation.

"Could we just go into Georgie's place and talk quietly?"
she asked.

Schmitty kept firm control on his lips, but have you ever
seen a man's eyes grin? There'd never been any hope that he
wouldn't notice the "Georgie."

"If Georgie has no objections," he said.

"No objections," I growled.

We went in and settled down.

"I don't want to accuse anybody," Lolly repeated, "especially now when I know how awful it is to be accused or
even suspected. My poor Eric."

"If you know anything, Mrs. Gibbons," Schmitty nudged.

"Nothing that everybody else doesn't know," she said,

"but nobody else will say anything because they all have it fixed in their minds that my Eric . . ." She left the rest of that unsaid. Obviously she couldn't bring herself to put it into words. "Everybody is just so certain," she resumed, "that Jill Armitage was killed by mistake. Suppose it wasn't a mistake, Inspector, but just made to look like one."

"How would that be done, Mrs. Gibbons? Somebody dressed Mrs. Armitage in one of Mrs. Hobbes' robes in preparation for shooting her?"

Lolly scowled.

"You think I'm a fool," she said. "Everybody thinks I'm a fool."

She said it with no bitterness, only in resignation. It was a simple fact, an obstacle she recognized and would have to surmount. She made me feel as though I were seeing her for the first time and hearing her speak for the first time. She had sloughed off all her little doll-baby ways and had somehow come up with a sensible woman she had been keeping buried under that overlay of simpering and fluttering.

"Just made to look like a mistake," Schmitty prompted. "Suppose you begin by explaining what you mean by that."

She explained and there was nothing new there. It was what we'd already had from Attorney Brennan and from Eric and his father. Nobody denied that Eric had shot the hawk, but, as the others had, she insisted that it was all he had done. Everything that followed had been set up to cash in on Eric's one misdemeanor. Anyone who for any reason wanted to do some shooting in our garden could go right ahead with it in the comfortable assurance that the blame would fall on her poor Eric.

"And the poor boy helped," she said. "He didn't know he was helping, but he did help."

She went into detail on that. Deprived of his ammunition and left with three unloaded weapons, he had been doing the only thing left open for him to do. He had been doing what she quoted him as calling "dry runs." For hours on end he had been standing at a window of his room with his rifle, sighting it on various objects in the garden and squeezing the trigger to slam the hammer into the emptiness of the unloaded chamber.

I was reminded of army days and rifle training. I recalled the unending boredom of dry-run days on the rifle range and for a moment I boggled at the thought that Eric Gibbons might have found the pursuit comforting or entertaining or anything but an insupportable tedium. Then I reminded myself that I was not Eric Gibbons. I was not and had never been a gun nut.

"People must have seen him there at his window," she continued. "You can imagine what it looked like."

"Like rehearsal in preparation for the real thing," Schmitty said.

"That's what I mean by his helping. It looked as though he was at least dreaming of shooting at that Hobbes woman. So, if someone wanted to get rid of Jill Armitage, someone who hated her and feared her, what a wonderful opportunity. It could be done and nobody would look beyond my Eric, and even if they did, nobody would look for people who were Jill Armitage's enemies. They would be too busy looking at the Hobbes woman's enemies."

"Mrs. Armitage had enemies?" Schmitty asked.

"Not a woman around here that didn't hate her, and most of them were afraid of her," Lolly said, as by imperceptible degrees she began resuming her old Lollypop overlay. "Every woman except her bosom friend, Daphne Hobbes, and she didn't care because she didn't have a husband. I never liked Jill. I'll admit that, but I was the only wife around here that wasn't afraid of her. I'm lucky. Mr. Gibbons isn't that kind of a man and we don't have that kind of a marriage."

By the time she had come to the last of that, she had the

whole of her silly surface back on. She didn't want to accuse
anybody. Instead she was spreading her accusations so
broadly that she had reduced them to something approaching nonsense. Maybe she did have the kind of husband and
the kind of marriage she was boasting about, but the way I
saw it, she'd had nothing to fear from Jill Armitage because
her Tootsie Roll had too patently not been Jill's type.

In Sylvia Weller's opinion, of course, anything with balls
was Jill Armitage's type, but that had always been an exag-
geration. At parties, for achieving the happy situation of
being hip deep in male admirers, Jill would try to surround
herself with everything that in voice was of lower range
than alto, but not every man she wanted to orbit her at parties was a man she would welcome in her bedroom.

I could think of a wife who might have been contemp-
tuous of Jill Armitage but who would never have bothered
to hate her and who would never have feared her. That was
Clara Grassi. Mike is one of those guys who is total catnip in
his effect on women, but I'll lay bets it's never given Clara
an uneasy moment. They're that kind of people and they do
have that kind of marriage.

"You're suggesting that Mrs. Armitage was killed by a
jealous wife," Schmitty said. "Killed because she made a
play for another woman's husband?"

"A successful play."

That was as far as she would move in the direction of anything specific. The inspector tried to push her.

"We're talking about murder, Mrs. Gibbons. You can't
hold back on anything you know."

"I don't know anything," she said.

"Then what are you talking about?"

"I'm talking about what I know, and that is that with the
kind of a woman Jill Armitage was and the way she
behaved, you can find people around here with far better
reasons for wanting her dead than the reason you think my

Eric had for wanting Mrs. Hobbes dead, and it's Jill who's been killed, and not Mrs. Hobbes."

In her own way and obviously without knowing it she was now talking Inspector Schmidt's language. Long before this I had recognized what he was prone to do in approaching the formation of a hypothesis and, recognizing it, I gave him the scholarly name for it. The inspector, however, had on his own discovered the principle first enunciated by William Occam. Occam's Razor was never far from his thinking. Given a choice of hypotheses he was a firm believer in concentrating on the less complicated one. Now Lollypop, of all people, was suggesting to him that it was the thing he should have been doing in this case.

"That, Mrs. Gibbons, is good thinking," he said. "Unfortunately, thinking without a few facts to think about isn't going to do any of us much good. You have no facts?"

"Only the way Jill Armitage was and the way she was always carrying on."

"Carrying on with whom?"

"With every man in sight."

"And to her carrying on different men reacted differently. Suppose you give me a suggestion, a few names, people I can look at, husbands who reacted in a way that disturbed their wives. If you know of a wife who has been violently disturbed, that might be even better."

"I don't know. I mind my own business, and now I wish I hadn't, but you can check around. It's different with you. It is your business, isn't it?"

So there it was. It was all she gave and I could see where it might well have been all she had to give. On what I've been telling you, you may have formed the impression that we people who shared the garden shared one another's lives as well, that we were a close-knit group doing all our partying together and popping in on our neighbors' houses constantly and casually.

Our setup would indicate it. We didn't lock our doors against our neighbors, and I have been telling you about group gatherings. To set the picture straight I should explain that our habit of locking nothing but our street doors had never in any of our minds stood as an invitation for the neighbors to drop in on us. It represented nothing but the fact that we had always trusted one another and part of that trust consisted of counting on everyone having sufficient respect for privacy so that we could expect that they would stay out without being locked out.

There were exceptions, of course. I, for example, had a closer relationship with Clara and Mike Grassi and their boys than I had with any of the other people. We did drop in on each other quite casually. I've told you how Mike was likely to be in and out of my place and similarly I had no inhibitions against dropping in on them anytime at all. I wasn't in the habit of doing that with any of the other neighbors and, so far as I knew, the Grassis did it with nobody but me.

That there were other relationships of that sort around the garden I've never doubted. Jill Armitage and Daphne Hobbes, for instance, had taken to doing it one with the other during the brief interval between the dead-hawk party and Jill's moving in on Daphne.

In the partying department, a lot of the people had asked me to doings in their houses and a lot of them had been in my place. Not all of them had included me in their parties and not all of them had been entertained by me. We all knew one another as neighbors but beyond that any kind of intimacy depended on individual compatibilities.

In all the time I had been living there I can recall only the one party that was set up as a gathering of all the residents and that's the one you already know about, the champagne binge Daphne Hobbes threw to give us the bird.

So when I say that what Lollypop Gibbons had handed

the inspector might have been all that she had to give, I am thinking that Lollypop and Tootsie Roll and their loutish son were unique. They were the people nobody liked. All of us knew them as neighbors. Everybody was correctly neighborly, but nobody had allowed himself to grow closer to them. Gossip, therefore, that might have been exchanged between some of us would hardly have been exchanged with Lollypop. You don't swap confidences with someone you are holding at arm's length.

If she did know anything more than she had told Inspector Schmidt, it would have to be only something she might have seen or might have overheard. They had been, you must remember, Jill's tenants and Jill, when occupying her own place, had lived right over their heads. It was more than possible that they'd been having grandstand seats for the observation of the comings and goings of any lovers Jill had been entertaining. It was no less than possible that in the event that an enraged wife had stormed up to Jill's place and screamed accusations and threats, Lollypop could have soaked up an earful.

Apart from such possibilities, however, it was unlikely that she could have been in possession of any facts that she could have passed on to the inspector.

VIII

"Does she know anything?" Schmitty asked me after she left. "Or was it just desperate reaching?"

"She's right about the way Jill carried on. It's possible that she doesn't know anything more specific."

I developed for the inspector the social picture I've just explored for you.

"Do you know any more?" Schmitty asked.

"A little."

"So give."

"Jill had flirtations all over the place, but you know how that is. A wife is likely to be irritated, but mostly those things come to nothing. Among the people around here, I know of only one husband with whom it was more serious. This one guy did actually score with her and his wife didn't like it; but if that poor woman ever took off against all the babes he's had on the mattress, you'd be working on the biggest mass murder in the history of crime."

"Names?"

"Weller. Gus Weller and wife Sylvia."

"I met them at the wake?"

"They were there."

"You know them," Schmitty said. "Do you have an opinion?"

I had an opinion.

"While it was going on, Sylvia was mad enough and anguished enough for anything, but the affair went cold some time ago and, just on Gus's track record, by now there has to be some other woman somewhere who is Sylvia's current grief. I can't quite see her reaching back into history to work on an old score."

"Suppose this one hit her specially hard. He's unfaithful. Okay, it's chronic. Still, every time it happens it does hurt. What hurts worst, though, is that it's happening this close to home, right here under the eyes of all the neighbors. That's not just the chronic humiliation. It's a special humiliation."

"But while it was going on she did nothing."

"That's the big question," Schmitty said. "You know her. Does she strike you as the kind of woman who might bide her time, save it till she had the right circumstances for settling accounts with what looked like no risk of getting caught? She's just aching to knock Armitage off and the ache won't go away. But there's nothing she can do about it, not with any hope of safety. Then Eric kills the bird. Hobbes raises hell about it. Armitage goes across to live with Hobbes. One night she walks around the place wearing one of her hostess' robes. The setup is just too good. Now it can be done and nobody'll think anything but Eric Gibbons. Before it's been motive and no opportunity and now opportunity has dropped into her lap. Opportunity has moved in and joined up with motive. She finds it irresistible. How about that?"

"I don't know," I said. "I can't see Sylvia Weller for it. One quick moment of rage, that would be possible for her. Planning and waiting and weighing risks just doesn't seem in character. Also, I don't think she'd have the guts. It wasn't the safe deal you're describing. One night out in the garden she methodically shoots a hole in each of Daphne's windows. She has to get out to the garden with a gun. She has to do all that shooting and she has to get back into her house unseen. Then the next night out again to hang around in the garden with a gun waiting on the chance that Jill will be wandering within range."

Schmitty broke in on me.

"And also on the chance that when and if she does she'll be wearing something of Daphne's and not something of her own." He added "No. Waiting out in the garden with a loaded rifle, there's no way to make that work. It has to be waiting inside and watching from a window. Where do the Wellers live?"

"Across the way, alongside the Hobbes house."

"No good," Schmitty said. "The shot was fired from this room or from just outside that garden door of yours. It had to be somebody on this side and somebody who could watch from a window, spot Armitage heading for the bar, and make it to right here in the couple of moments it took her to start pouring her drink. That means someone out of this house or right next door, not much further off than that."

"Okay," I said. "The Grassis upstairs, me, the Gibbonses next door, and Jill's tenant, Jackson, above them. By the way, he's another reason I can't make it jell for Sylvia Weller."

Schmitty jumped at that.

"She found a better way of getting even?" he asked, and now he was eager. "Giving her husband as good as she got? Having an affair of her own and having it here on the home ground where she could humiliate him the way he humiliated her?"

I had to laugh. For uptight, puritanical Sylvia Weller, the picture was too funny and, apart from that, I could see no reason why the inspector should be so avid to grab at the idea. How could he possibly think that would get him anywhere?

"Sylvia?" I said. "Not on your life. Her motto is *nolo me tangere*. She wears it written in letters of fire across her brow: 'Don't touch me.' That could be part of the reason why Gus is always on the prowl for other beds."

Schmitty was reluctant to give it up.

"You never can be sure about people in things like that," he said. "Her husband's not coming home nights. He's getting his some place else and she's getting hers upstairs next door. From her lover's window she can watch the house across the way. It puts her in perfect position."

"There's a complication you don't know about," I said.

"Like what?"

"Jill Armitage was between husbands. She had zeroed in on Jack Jackson for her next and he was showing all the signs of responding."

"Jackson was scoring with her?"

"She had rented him her place and she moved in with Daphne. It was only a matter of time before she'd be moving back home. They were on the way."

"Then I'd better talk to him," Schmitty said. "See what he can tell me."

"He wasn't fighting it," I said.

"He was intimate with the dead woman. It's always possible he knows something and he's so sure that that kid, Eric, killed her that he just hasn't brought anything else to mind. He could even be surprised at how much he knows and hasn't thought of."

I did recognize the possibility, but I couldn't see it as the great opening Inspector Schmidt evidently felt I had given him. Relaxed alone with me, he had, of course, kicked off his shoes. Now he was climbing into them and without even wincing. That never happens unless he is so convinced that he is at the very edge of coming up with something hot that anticipation has him anaesthetized. He wasn't waiting to take the long way around, out to the street and over next door to ring Jackson's doorbell.

With the inspector leading the way, we took the short cut, out to the garden and up the outside stairs next door to Jackson's flower-bedecked balcony. The door to his living room stood ajar. Schmitty knocked on it. There was no response. He called Jackson's name. No response. He shouted. Nothing from inside, but his shouting brought us Tim Clancy. Tim came trotting up the stairs from the garden.

"Want the guy, Inspector?" he asked.

"I want to talk to him."

"Not home. We haven't been in here because, when we got to it, he wasn't around. So we did other places first. A lot of the people are talking about how they won't feel safe in their houses here until we arrest somebody. Maybe he's so scared he did more than just talk about it, like he took off to go beddy-bye some place else where maybe the bogeyman can't get him."

"How long since you first tried to find him?" Schmitty asked.

"Hours," Clancy answered. "You know, Inspector, when that nephew was here, the second one who yelled around about wanting to know where his aunt had gone because she needed him to protect her?"

"Yes?"

"Right after you got rid of him, we were ready to come in here for a look around and this guy was gone then."

"Then we'll take a look around without him," Schmitty said.

The door, after all, was standing ajar and I was a neighbor. There was nothing to stop us from dropping in.

I had it figured that Clancy had to be wrong. I was ready to take bets that Jackson was there and that we'd find him in the bedroom, corked off. None of us had been long asleep when the shot wakened us. I could guess that since then a lot of the neighbors had climbed back into the sack and were making up for lost rest. It didn't seem likely that the inspector's shouting wouldn't have wakened Jackson, no matter how soundly he slept, but I thought I had that figured as well. Jackson might well have chosen to ignore it, expecting that we would give up and go away and he could go back to sleep again.

I could imagine his thinking. Since nobody had shown any disposition to do what he thought should be done, since it was evident that Eric Gibbons would not be dragged out and hanged from one of the stouter trees in our garden, he probably felt that there was no reason for him to give up on his sleep just to piddle around ineffectually with a lot of official and unofficial bleeding hearts.

I filled the inspector in on my thinking. I felt that, before we looked around too much, it might be good form to try the bedroom and wake our unwitting host.

"Unless you think there's some reason for looking around without him," I said.

"No reason," the inspector said. "I can already see the housekeeping is terrific. He sure keeps a neat house."

I hadn't noticed, but once Schmitty had mentioned it, I did some looking around as we passed through the living room. It struck me then that it was Jill Armitage's room, totally and exclusively hers. I had been in that room other times, times when she had herself been in residence, and times when the place had been occupied by earlier tenants.

Those earlier tenants had been a varied lot, but each during his residence had had something of himself in the place. It might have been a pipe rack with his pipes in it or some framed photographs set about or a book or two he had been reading, something or other that indicated that Jill's room was being used by someone else. Now there was nothing, Jill's stuff and nothing more.

Since I was the one who knew the layout, I led the way to the bedroom. There it was more of the same. It was Jill's bedroom, nothing in sight to indicate that Jackson was in residence, not even Jackson himself. I had guessed wrong on that. The bed was empty and all neatly made up with the spread on it for the day.

Looking it over, Schmitty whistled. He made a dive for the bedroom closet and pulled the door open. I looked and I whistled. The closet was empty. Nothing on the hangers, nothing on the shelves. If anything had been in there, it had been cleaned out.

Now Schmitty and Clancy were working together and with every moment the look on Inspector Schmidt's face was more grim and with every moment there was something more ominous in the way he carried himself. There was a storm building. Heads were about to roll.

They pulled open bureau drawers. They covered the whole place, trying all the closets, all the drawers, and everywhere it was the same. Nothing anywhere. Not a change of socks, a change of shirt, a change of underwear. Nothing.

"Can a guy just live in the clothes he stands up in?" Tim Clancy asked.

It may have been a rhetorical question. In any case, I answered it.

"He doesn't," I said. "He changes clothes as much as anybody else does. I've been seeing him around. Different color shirts. Different ties. Three or four sports jackets. Different slacks. A couple of suits."

"And he packed it all up," Schmitty growled. "He packed it all up and walked out of here with it. He walked out past all the smart cops we've got watching outside. Maybe they even flagged him a cab and helped him load his suitcases."

Storming downstairs and out to the street, Schmitty had fire in his eye. With frozen control he questioned the officer stationed outside. Yes, the man had been at his post. Yes, he had seen Jackson leave. He couldn't set the time exactly, but his approximation was a good fit to Clancy's. It looked as though Jackson had only just pulled out when Clancy had first tried to find him.

"And you let him go?"

"My orders, Inspector, sir, were to stop any strangers coming out and to stop anybody, resident or stranger, if he came out carrying anything. No packages go out without opening them and inspecting them."

"And he opened his suitcases and you inspected them and they had nothing in them but his clothes. So they were all right. Nothing to worry about. He's just a fussy guy who won't spend even one night in a bad neighborhood like this, a neighborhood where women get murdered?"

The poor cop broke out in a sweat under the lash of the inspector's sarcasm, but he stood his ground.

"I knew he wasn't a stranger, Inspector, sir," he said. "I seen him inside. I knew he was a resident. He didn't come out carrying anything, no suitcases, nothing."

Schmitty was silent for what seemed like an infinite string of eternities. He just stood there looking at that cop. The poor fellow was young, only barely past the minimum age for the force, and that's not too much more than a boy. I had to admire the way he stood up under that scrutiny. I wouldn't have wanted to face it.

As it prolonged itself, however, it did become easier. The inspector's grimness didn't evaporate, but gradually it did go through a change. The hard edge came off it. When he spoke again the anger had gone out of his voice. Now there was nothing in the sound of it but patience.

"Your orders weren't as good as they should have been, officer," he said. "They should have specified that anyone moving out bag and baggage was to be stopped. So it's not your fault."

"Bag and baggage, Inspector, sir," the kid said. "I wouldn't have known what I had ought to do about that. I'd have held him and asked for instructions."

"You're not covering yourself," Schmitty told him, "but it's no better covering for your sergeant on the orders he gave you. It's important for me to know. He came out carrying nothing just like he wasn't doing anything but going off for a walk because all hell was breaking loose inside and he wasn't going to get any sleep anyway?"

"Yes, Inspector, sir, just like that, except that he wasn't walking. He got in his car and pulled away."

"Not that there's any reason why you should have," Schmitty said, "but, did you just happen to notice the license number on his car?"

"It wasn't his, sir. It had a Z license."

"All right, a hired car. So you did notice the license. Remember the number?"

"I'm sorry, sir. I didn't take any notice of the number, Inspector. You see, sir, standing out here and the car parked right in front, I noticed the tires. None of them were good, but the near front, that one was real bad. I wouldn't want to ride on it, not even from here to the corner. I couldn't figure anyone even thinking to ride on rubber like that. Thinking about that, I noticed the license and I was telling myself there ought to be a law on them car-rental people. They hadn't ought to ever let a car go out like that. It can be murder."

The boy wasn't unobservant. It was just bad luck that he had concentrated on observing the wrong things.

Inspector Schmidt takes what he can get. Since this officer had been interested in the car, Schmitty questioned him about that. He got the make, the model, the year, the color, and again the condition of the tires.

So there was nothing for it but to put out an alarm for Jack Jackson. While the inspector was setting that up, I did some thinking. I remembered that it so happened that I had been going out just at the time when Jackson had arrived to take up residence. I had witnessed his arrival and he had arrived exactly as the young cop was saying he had departed. He had come without luggage, without even the smallest parcel.

I had thought nothing of it at the time. I suppose I assumed that he had already sent his things over or would be bringing them over later. That I had never seen them arrive hadn't made me think at all. As you already know, in our little corner of the big city any looking out we do is likely to be done at the garden side of our houses. Comings and goings on the street side might just in passing be noticed, as I had noticed Jackson's arrival, but I was ready to say that nobody kept any watch out there.

On the other hand, as I had already told the inspector, Jackson did have clothes, at least as many changes as your average reasonably affluent man-about-town will have.

For what it was worth, I filled the inspector in on my recollections. Hanging on my every word, he heard me out. When I had finished, he summed it up.

"His coming in is unimportant," he said. "He brought his stuff over here sometime when you didn't happen to see him. It's when he got his stuff out that matters. Sometime yesterday? It could have been anytime after he last changed clothes. Maybe somebody happened to see him come out and load up. It's my guess that nobody did. He probably did it gradually, never at any time carrying out enough to be noticed. Suppose every time he changed clothes he got those things he'd changed out of here."

"Like a hotel deadbeat preparing to skip his bill?" I said.

"Except that he wouldn't be running out on his bill," Schmitty said. "He was preparing to kill. He was going to run out on the accounting he'd be owing the law."

I had trouble making sense of that.

"A hotel can hold a man's property against his unpaid bill," I said. "Holding a man's shirts and pants and socks against his paying for a woman's life would hardly work out for anything."

"If we had anything that belonged to him," Schmitty explained, "it might lead to an identification. It could be a help in tracking him down. I've put everything we've got into working the apartment and five gets you ten the boys'll find nothing, not even a partial print."

I shook my head but not in negation. I was trying to shake the fog out of it. With every moment I was falling into deeper confusion.

"But he didn't just kill and run," I mumbled, talking more to myself than to the inspector. "He hung around for at least a couple of hours. He was over at Daphne's when you got here and he stayed over there along with all the others. What would that have been for? Since he was skipping in any case, why did he wait and take extra risks?"

"He was that confident. He thought he had it open-and-shut against Eric Gibbons. We'd grab the kid and that would be the end of it."

"If he was counting on that, then why did he work so hard at fixing the apartment so he could make a quick getaway out of it and leave behind no trace of himself? I don't see how we can have it both ways."

"He saw exactly how it could be both ways. He's a planner and he's smart. He was prepared for the quick, leave-no-trace-behind getaway because he had no way of knowing he wouldn't run into a patch of bad luck. Somebody walks out into the garden at the wrong moment and sees him with the gun, anything like that. He prepared for that. Then he thought it had gone so well that he didn't need it and so badly that he had to hang around for a while."

"Badly for him? How?"

"He got the wrong woman. It was all for nothing. He hung on just on the chance that he could somehow still get at Mrs. Hobbes."

"Oh, come on. If it had been Eric, you could assume he had meant to get Daphne Hobbes. If it had been Sylvia Weller, you could assume that she meant to get Jill Armitage. If it's Jackson, there's no way of knowing which of them he was after. Aren't you completely in the dark there? Motive unknown?"

"In the dark on his motive, certainly," the inspector conceded, "but not on his intended victim. Geography and history give us that. He rented the apartment from which he could draw a bead on the Hobbes house."

"He didn't shoot from the apartment," I reminded Schmitty. "You established that from the beginning. It was a level shot, not fired from above."

"He rented the apartment from which he could watch the Hobbes house and from which he could get downstairs quickly and fire his shot from the best place there was for making it look like Eric's work. It was the perfect location from which to take a shot at Daphne Hobbes. It was no good at all for going after Mrs. Armitage."

Elaborating on that, Inspector Schmidt cleared it up for me. There could have been no way for Jackson to know that if he rented Jill's apartment, she would move across the garden and settle in on Daphne Hobbes. She might have moved anywhere. She might have gone off on a trip. How could he have known she would move into perfect range?

"He could have expected to know where she moved," I argued. "She'd have to tell him where he was to send the rent, if nothing else."

"And that could have been to her lawyers or a bank. But let's say he would know where he could go to find her. Would that be any place where he could hide behind the suspicion that would automatically fall on Eric Gibbons?"

He had me there. I hadn't thought of that.

"Okay for the geography," I conceded. "You also said history."

"For some reason he's out to get Mrs. Hobbes," Schmitty explained. "It's a good guess that he's keeping an eye on her, watching her movements, looking for a chance to get at her.

He has an eye out for any information he can pick up on her."

He didn't have to lay out any more of it for me.

"The dead-hawk thing," I said. "He saw Jill's gossip piece and it was just what he needed. It gave him his set-up. Our houses all open on the garden. A stupid kid playing with a rifle, shooting a bird in the garden. Daphne gets the kid in trouble. All Jackson has to do is get in here, make some moves to lay foundations for the strongest possible case against Eric, and do what he came for."

"Right," Schmitty said. "So now it's to talk to your friend Daphne. She's got to have some idea on who would want her dead."

I tried to fit that into the pattern and I couldn't.

"But she didn't know Jackson until after he moved in here," I said. "It wasn't until Jill introduced them. I'm certain of that. It doesn't work, Schmitty. If she knows somebody is out to murder her and she knows it's Jackson, she is going to have some reaction to his moving in across the way and it won't be just a lot of happy dithering about the way he's improved her view by putting all those pretty flowering shrubs out on the balcony."

The inspector grabbed at that. For him it was yet another goody.

"The plants on the balcony? They're his?"

"First thing he did on moving in."

"What kind did Armitage have out there before? Smaller ones? Lower ones?"

"None at all. Nobody ever thought of flowers on the balconies. You can see there aren't any on the others. After all, there is the garden. Daphne enjoyed looking across at his flowers, but for my money they were superfluous."

"Not for a guy who wanted to lurk behind them with a rifle waiting for his victim to come into range."

Another piece clicking into place, but my question still stood unanswered.

"But he wasn't anyone she knew," I repeated.

Inspector Schmidt shrugged it off. "He couldn't be," he said. "It won't be the first time a man doesn't do his own killing. People start doing that, it'll put all the hired guns out of business. Jackson has a contract on her. Why not?"

I laughed but it was rueful.

"Not the first time I asked a stupid question," I said.

"If our case isn't going to fall on its face, it has to answer all the questions."

"Including the stupid ones?"

"When a jury leaves the box to start its deliberations," Schmitty said, "you can't get into every juror's head to sort out the good questions from the stupid ones. If you can, you should have them empty of all questions."

"And I serve my purpose. I keep you up on what a stupid juror might get to thinking."

"I'm a pro, Baggy, and you are not," the inspector said. "We can call you a semipro. You keep me up on how things might look to an amateur and that's what the jury system is all about. Jurors are amateurs."

And so are witnesses. It can be that even a good witness knows more than he's aware of. It had been that way with me and the flowering plants Jackson had installed on the balcony. Now we had another demonstration of that phenomenon. Before pulling out to go have a talk with Daphne Hobbes, the inspector did a quick round of the neighbors. He was looking for someone who might have seen Jackson when he came in with luggage or went out with luggage.

Nobody could help him. I was the only one who had witnessed his first arrival and, as you know, he had then been empty-handed. People had seen him take deliveries, but those were all of a nature that could be of no interest to Schmitty.

Newspapers. Liquor. Small grocery orders. That sort of minor day-to-day stuff and nothing more.

Clara Grassi had seen some of that.

"What I'm interested in," Schmitty told her, "is something different. Suitcases. Sizable boxes. Maybe laundry deliveries or pickups. Dry-cleaner deliveries. Packages that might have been clothes."

Clara shook her head. At least she began, but then she stopped short and her eyes widened.

"There was something funny," she murmured.

"You did see something?" Schmitty was eager.

Clara wasn't to be hurried. She was thinking.

Schmitty tried pushing her.

"It doesn't matter if it seems crazy," he said. "It doesn't matter if you don't understand it. Just tell me. Maybe we can work it out together."

"There were times," Clara said, "when I saw him go out and I'd happen to notice what he was wearing. A brown suit, say, and a yellow shirt, brownish tie." She hesitated, blushing a bit. "When I'm doing things in the kitchen," she explained, "I like to work by the window. I like to look out and see people come by. Mike teases me about it. He says I'm small-town and I've never gotten over it."

"You watched when he came and went?"

This was just what the inspector wanted.

"Not watched," Clara said in demurral. "Not him especially. It was just that I'd be at the kitchen window looking out and it was just what I happened to see, anyone who came by."

"I understand, but you did see him go and come?"

"Some of the time I did. I'd see him go out that way, say in the brown, and then a little while later I'd see him come in again and he'd changed. Gray suit, blue shirt, blue tie. Like that."

Schmitty grinned.

"So it's your impression that he didn't do like other people," he summed up. "He didn't come home to change his clothes. He went out to change his clothes. That can be the answer. He had another place where he kept his things. He wasn't ever living in the Armitage apartment. He was just using it as a stakeout."

Clara shuddered. "I never thought of it that way," she said. "I thought I knew what he was doing. I guess that's why I took notice of his changes. Before we were married Mike used to live that way."

"What way?"

The question was mine. I could make no sense of what she said. To me it sounded as though she were suggesting that before they were married Mike had been shacking up with her and would go home to his own place only to change his clothes. I know people who could tell me something of that sort without startling me in the least, but never Clara Grassi. As Mike would tell her, Clara was small-town and she had always been small-town, delightfully and incorrigibly so.

She explained. "Mike would leave his office," she said. "He would be coming around to pick me up for a date. On his way, he stopped in a store and bought a shirt. Then he stopped in at the dry cleaners and there he changed out of the suit he'd been wearing and left it to be pressed and he'd put on another suit he'd left there before for pressing. While he was there he changed into the new shirt and he just left the one he'd taken off. Walked away from it, abandoned it. He was always doing that, instead of taking the pressed suit home or letting them deliver it. And shirts? I don't know that he ever had a shirt laundered. He kept walking away from them after he'd worn them a day. He said that's the way bachelors live."

"Maybe rich bachelors," Schmitty said, "or crazy ones."

"Back then before we were married," Clara continued,

"things didn't cost what they cost today, but still it was the craziest kind of extravagance. His suits got more wear from the pressing than from being on his back, and all the time walking away from perfectly good shirts. I put a stop to that."

By the time we were having this talk with Clara Grassi, day had come. The normal world was beginning to stretch and wake, readying itself to go about its Sunday morning pursuits. I hadn't had anything that came close to a proper night's sleep but I wasn't feeling the lack of it. I was too hopped up to think about sleep, but I was thinking about a shave and a shower. I didn't dare let myself think about breakfast. I knew that if I once let it enter my head, I was not going to be able to think about anything else.

Schmitty was all set to take right off with the questions he now had for Daphne Hobbes. I made a stab at slowing him down.

"She'll be asleep," I told him. "She had a broken night."

Schmitty looked at his watch. It was still early enough to give him pause.

"Jackson's on the loose," he mumbled.

"He doesn't know where she is," I argued. "He was here for quite a while after she left. It's not as though there were any possibility that he followed them when she went off with nephew Gordon."

"I wouldn't want to underestimate him," Schmitty fretted.

He settled for telephoning and alerting the man he'd sent with her and Gordon Hobbes. He could have been happier if the man had seen Jackson and would have known him on sight, but he did what he could with a description.

I got my shower and shave and the inspector, since he was holding off in any case, took over the bathroom as soon as I was out of it. I rattled around in the kitchen, making preliminary stabs at trying to pull together some kind of breakfast for us, but Clara sent Mike down to tell me to drop it. Anytime we were ready, we were to come back upstairs and she would have a proper breakfast for us. Clara never could believe that a bachelor would be any more competent about making coffee than, in her opinion, he would be about taking care of his clothes.

With my feet under the Grassi table and my nose reaching out for the perfumes of Clara's coffee and Clara's pancakes, I couldn't think she wasn't right. Even Inspector Schmidt showed awareness of what he was putting into his mouth. When he's hot on an investigation, he seems to live on lunch-counter coffee and lunch-counter gelid apple pie and he never notices the horror of what he's ingesting.

We ate more and we drank more coffee than I like to admit to. When the inspector called time, I was beyond having any regrets. I couldn't have held any more.

Before we took off, Schmitty made one stop. He checked in with the men he had working the apartment Jackson had been tenanting so peculiarly. They were still working on the place, but they had gone far enough with it to have formed a good idea of what they could expect to find in the areas that were still to be done.

"Nothing, Inspector," the fingerprint men reported. "This is a guy who lives in gloves."

"Or did a professional wipe-up of the whole damn place," Schmitty muttered.

"How could he?" I asked. "He had no time. He was out with the rest of us right after the shooting. He was in the garden or over at Daphne's from that time right on down to when he took off. If he was in here as much as five minutes all told between Jill's murder and the time he skipped out on us, it was a lot."

"What about the time he had before the shooting?" Schmitty asked. "He had everything prepared. He wiped the whole place clean and then he sat here with his gun, waiting, but like an old-fashioned gentleman, fully dressed and with his gloves on. He saw what he thought he was waiting for, nipped down the stairs, stood outside your door, fired his shot, slung the gun into your living room, pocketed his gloves, and went back up to his place to go through his apartment and out to the street and away."

I caught it.

"But before he could even have made it up the stairs," I said, "he would have heard Daphne screaming and he would have known he had muffed it. He'd shot the wrong woman."

"Right. Upstairs he shed his jacket and tie, pulled out of his socks, and ran back down like he'd just hauled on his shirt and pants like anyone else to go across the garden and help Mrs. Hobbes."

"And when he decided it was time to leave," I added, "he just went back up to the apartment, picked up the tie and the jacket he had lying ready for a grab in passing, and put them on while he was going downstairs to the street."

"Nothing could have been easier. For standing by with Mrs. Hobbes he looked no more dressed than the rest of you. He was wearing only what he could have yanked on in a hurry when he heard the shot, but dressing the rest of the way was no more than he could do just while he was passing through the apartment and going down the stairs to the street."

"A little more than that," I said, remembering something I thought I'd noticed. "He would need to have stopped to put on socks and shoes. Over at Daphne's he was like the rest of us, only bedroom slippers on bare feet."

"Not exactly like the rest of you," Schmitty corrected me. "No socks. You're right about that, but not bedroom slippers. Street shoes, a pair of loafers. I noticed that but not to make anything of it. There are guys who don't bother to own bedroom slippers."

"Even so," I said, "it would have been the same thing, getting out of slippers and pulling on socks and shoes or getting out of loafers to put on socks and get back into loafers."

"Did he need socks?" Schmitty asked. "Just for going past the officer down in the street and jumping into his rented car? Would the officer notice he had no socks on or think anything of it if he did notice?"

As usual, Inspector Schmidt was way ahead of me. One of the fashions taken up by the young was going sockless even when shod. If the cop had noticed, he would have dismissed it as a case of arrested development, like the white-fringed baldheads who have taken to letting their fringes grow down to their shoulders.

IX

On the way over to see Daphne and her nephews another question popped into my head. I didn't for a moment think it would be unanswerable. It was just that it had me stopped. I expected that the inspector would have already thought of it and that he would have the answer. He had, of course, and he did.

It was the rifle. At one time or another he must have brought it to the apartment. Since it had turned up under my windowseat, there was no problem about how he had carried it away. He hadn't done that, but how did he get it there? Jill had rented him the apartment furnished but it wasn't possible that a rifle would have been among the furnishings.

Inspector Schmidt gave it no thought.

"Easy," he said. "That never was a problem. One time or another he came in carrying a long parcel. That nobody happens to have seen him do it means nothing. We have to assume that not every last one of his comings and goings was observed. Clara Grassi doesn't spend all her time at her kitchen window."

"True enough," I said. "She spends a lot of time out in the garden with the kids, and evenings, when Mike's home and the kids are in bed, she's with Mike."

"All of that and there are other things she does in other parts of the house, not to speak of the times she goes out. If Jackson was supercareful, he might have brought the rifle in late at night when there would have been the least chance of being seen."

"Yes," I said. "He would do that."

Schmitty didn't care about pinning it down. He felt he didn't need it.

"He had no reason for being careful about that," he said. "His plan didn't call for it. He could come in anytime carrying any kind of a package. Even if somebody saw him, it wouldn't matter. He was going to knock Mrs. Hobbes off and be gone. Nobody would be giving him a thought until afterward. He was never in the least interested in keeping us from thinking about him once he was gone. He's too smart not to have known that the simple facts would pinpoint him for us. He's the one who disappears right after the shooting and he's cleaned the apartment of even the smallest trace of anything that might have helped us find him. Not bringing any clothes in wasn't because he didn't want to be seen bringing stuff in. It was because he couldn't let himself be seen moving stuff out. Since he never planned to move the rifle out after the shooting, he had no problem there."

"He built all that suspicion against Eric Gibbons," I said, thinking aloud, "but he wasn't putting all his dependence on it. He had himself all set for his getaway in the event that the case against Eric didn't hold up."

"His plan didn't hang on the case against the Gibbons boy holding up," Schmitty said. "He had no way of guaranteeing that it would and he was smart enough to see that it was most unlikely that it would hold up. His plan grew out of knowing the first suspicion would light on Eric. He shot at the windows to build the suspicion up to the place where for a while nobody could be looking at anybody but Eric, and that was all he needed. What that was for was to give him time to be well away before we would even think of looking beyond Eric. He wasn't building a stone wall for me to come up against, only a barrier that would slow me down, and it worked. Didn't it just work?"

I made a stab at giving the situation a hopeful twist.

"If he's a hired gun," I suggested, "I saw him, you saw him, everybody saw him. A run through on the mug shots you have downtown . . ."

"That'll be routine," the inspector said, "but we can't expect it to get us anything. When they have a record and they have mug shots on file, only the stupidest ones set up a job like this where he has to show himself that openly and let that many people get to know him. If there's one thing we can be sure about on this baby, it's that he's not one of the stupid ones. We don't have them all. There's always new operators coming into the business. Jackson's got to be a first-timer."

"With that much expertise?"

"When I say first-timer," Schmitty explained, "it doesn't have to mean that he hasn't killed before. He probably has, and he's been getting away with it. What I mean is, when we get him it's likely going to be his first time arrested."

I liked that "when we get him." It was good that Inspector Schmidt should be going forward on this with enough confidence to say "when" and not "if," but beyond a blind faith in the inspector's skill and the inspector's acumen, I could see no grounds for optimism. I guess my doubts showed.

"Which is it, Baggy?" Schmitty asked. "Is the old cop getting pretty cocky or is he just whistling in the dark?"

"If it weren't you," I admitted, "I'd have to be thinking one or the other."

Schmitty grinned at me. "We're not that bad off," he said. "I'm not going to have to pull him out of a hat. We've got Mrs. Hobbes and there are two ways she could be able to do it for us. What I'm hoping is that it will be the better way."

"She'll come up with a list of people Jackson could be working for?"

"A list if it has to be," Schmitty said. "I'll be happier if she can pin it down to one enemy."

"And the second way?" I asked.

"He got the wrong woman," Schmitty reminded me. "That means the contract is still out on Daphne Hobbes. You're not betting he won't try again?"

"You're not betting he'll muff it the second time and you'll catch him on his second try?" I countered. "It could be after he's brought it off."

"Not after, Baggy," Schmitty growled, "before. We'll have to get to him when he starts moving in. It's not as though now we won't know what we're looking for."

That seemed to me not much more than a hope. I can't say I was enamored of it, but there was no need for me to put my feeling into words. The inspector had already said that he preferred the first way.

He so much preferred it that he dug and dug, going after it with everything he had. Daphne was holed up in a hotel suite. A cop was stationed outside the door and inside she had her nephew with her. That was the blood-kin nephew, Roderick Pagnell. The other one, Gordon Hobbes, was not in evidence. It seemed reasonable enough. Since there were the two of them, they could spell each other.

We couldn't have been more welcome. The nephew took us calmly, but Daphne was overjoyed. I think she had hoped that we'd come to tell her that Inspector Schmidt had the whole thing wrapped up and she could come out of hiding. Although he did have to disappoint her on that score, the disappointment appeared to be something less than shattering.

We were there and for her that seemed to be sufficient cause for joy. Shut up with Roderick Pagnell, she was on the edge of exploding with boredom and irritation. We were company and, better still, we seemed to be company that was to her liking.

"Gordon had to nip off," she explained. "I hated to see him go, but he insisted that he did have to change his clothes. I suppose it was necessary. In New York one cannot go about in full daylight in a tail coat and an opera hat. One would have to be a circus ringmaster. I appreciate that, but I can't understand why he would have to be the other side of forever about it."

"It doesn't matter, Aunt Daphne," Pagnell told her. "You have me."

He might have done better if he'd said nothing.

"You're so right, my good Rick," she purred at him. "You're so right. I do have you. I have you up to here." She indicated a level that was at about the middle of her forehead. "If these two charmers hadn't arrived in the very nick of time, I should have been finished. I was just about to go down for the third time."

"Aunt Daphne," Pagnell wailed his reproach.

"Nephew Rick." She mimicked his wail. "I do wish you could think of something amusing to do. Turn blue, for instance, and drop dead."

Wheeling away from her unfortunate blood-kin, she addressed herself to us.

"That's my favorite Americanism," she said. "I learned it eons ago from a cabbie and I've been waiting all this time for an opportunity to use it. Cabbies, of course, do have many opportunities."

Pagnell forced a laugh.

"Aunt Daph," he said, "you are a caution."

Daphne sighed.

"Inspector," she said, "I don't like to criticize, but you can see what you've been subjecting me to. A 'caution'? Nobody's been a caution since the Golden Jubilee. He can't even talk properly."

Having an audience for it, she could have gone on that way forever. She might even have begun enjoying poor Roderick. The inspector broke it up.

"You're going to have to help me, Mrs. Hobbes," he said.

"I doubt that I can, Inspector. You'll find I'm not at all the Miss Marple type."

I verified it later. Schmitty didn't have the faintest notion of who Miss Marple might be. He just sensed that she was irrelevant.

"What do you know about the man who calls himself Jack Jackson?"

"Gillian's tenant? Not much, Inspector, but before I tell you even the little I know, I must first see you out of your shoes." She turned to me. "See?" she said. "I do learn. I remembered this time that I wasn't to call them 'boots.'"

If making himself comfortable was a condition he would have to meet before he could have anything out of the lady, Inspector Schmidt was not the man to say her nay, certainly not when she was offering him the luxury of going shoeless. She went on with it, however, wanting to order up coffee for us or sherry or anything at all. The inspector had to fight off her hospitality to bring her back to Jackson.

"Jack Jackson," she said when Schmitty had settled her down. "He's a charmer, but I should say only for about the first hour or thereabouts. He soon becomes tiresome. No conversation. Poor Gillian never recognized it. She was enchanted with him. Of course, so far as looks go, he is a stunner. Smashingly handsome in a slightly vulgar way, but if a man has those looks, outstandingly beautiful, he will need just a touch of vulgarity to make him attractive. If you gentlemen won't find it offensive of me saying so, there is something peculiarly masculine about vulgarity."

Inspector Schmidt didn't mind. It was my guess that he had little notion of what she was talking about and that he cared even less. He had to steer her into more useful channels.

"When did you first meet him?"

"After Gillian let her apartment to him. When he moved in."

"Never before that? You had never seen him or known him before that? Please, think hard, Mrs. Hobbes."

"I suppose I'm being dull, but surely it can't be important."

"Murder is important, Mrs. Hobbes. The fact that he got Mrs. Armitage when he meant to get you makes it no less important. Right now, it makes it even more important. Part of my job is finding this man so he can stand trial for the killing he's done, but the other part of my job, and the more important part, is to secure him before he can rectify his mistake. I don't mean he can rectify it by bringing her back. We know that's impossible. I don't want him killing you, Mrs. Hobbes."

Daphne needed a moment or two for taking that in. She was blinking with astonishment.

"Jackson?" she gasped. "Jackson and not the loutish Gibbons boy. Of course, Jackson is something of a lout as well, but nevertheless . . ."

"Take my word for it, Mrs. Hobbes," Schmitty told her. "The evidence is strong. I'm ready to call it conclusive. Not all of it is in yet, but everything that comes in strengthens it and I don't see a chance that it can change. Jackson is our man."

"It's incredible but, since you say so, I do believe it. You've put the arm on him?"

She hadn't been depending exclusively on taxi drivers for learning her Americanisms. I had noticed it earlier. The real thing she had intermingled with some ersatz she had picked up from TV.

"I'm sorry, ma'am. I haven't. He's disappeared. We have an alarm out for him. We're looking."

Roderick muttered something that sounded like "incompetence," but one look from his aunt silenced him.

"A man I hardly knew," she said. "A man who hardly knew me. Such encounters as we'd had were nothing but amiable. He would have to be daft."

"Take it back before that, Mrs. Hobbes," the inspector urged. "He had only one reason for renting Mrs. Armitage's apartment. He didn't want it for a place to live in. It was the perfect place for what he needed, a place from which he could watch you and wait for his chance to kill you."

"Like a duck blind?" she asked.

Schmitty seemed hesitant about calling the lady a duck. I did it for him.

"You were the sitting duck, but he made a mistake, Daph. He bagged Jill."

She shook her head.

"Great trouble," she murmured, thinking aloud in her effort to make some sense of what the inspector was telling her. "Great expense and for what? To kill an old woman he didn't even know? One hears of men going out of their minds and going on a shooting rampage, just killing anybody who happens by. That's difficult enough to understand. But this? It's just not possible."

"You've hit it on the nose, Mrs. Hobbes," Schmitty told her. "It isn't possible. He would have to have had a reason. It doesn't need to be a good reason. It was good enough for him. That's why you must try to remember."

"There's nothing to remember," she insisted. "Old women can be forgetful. I know that, Inspector, but I don't think it's happened to me. I should think I would be aware of it if it had."

"What about money?" Pagnell asked.

"My money? Please, Rick, just this once you might try not

to be idiotic. I know it's an effort, but you must try. You know where the money is to go."

You wouldn't expect that her words would leave Roderick Pagnell looking smug and satisfied, but they did.

"I know where it is to go, Aunt Daphne," he said.

She snapped at him.

"You've always known," she said, "and it's no good sulking about it. My own mite will be yours. You're insufferable, but my late brother—God forgive him—did father you, and that's that."

Pagnell was working at something. In his determination to get it in he could let insult pass him by.

"I can't think the inspector would be interested in small bequests," he said.

"I can't think," she said, taking the words out of her nephew's mouth, "that the inspector is interested in any bequests. How could the first penny ever go to a complete stranger briefly in residence across the garden?"

"If we're thinking money," Inspector Schmidt said, "and we put it together with your being sure that Jackson came into your life only after he'd rented Mrs. Armitage's apartment, then we have to think he's a hired killer, killing for the fee he'll receive from the person who will benefit directly."

Daphne glared at Pagnell. It was a glare that read as clearly as any spoken words.

"See what you've started with your nonsense," it was saying.

Quickly, however, she turned the glare on the inspector and then she spoke as well.

"We are not thinking money," she said. "I will hear no more of that. It's ridiculous and it's disgusting. You're a sensible man, Inspector, and a clever one. Assuredly you have no time to waste on ill-natured nonsense."

The glare intimidated Roderick Pagnell. He fell silent and

moved to a window where he stood looking out. He hadn't come down with any sudden interest in the view. His face was contorted with fury and frustration. He couldn't be expected to be happy about leaving it out where we could look at it. The window was an excuse for turning his back on us.

Inspector Schmidt isn't so easily intimidated. Ignoring all warning signals, he spoke.

"I have my job to do," he said. "Don't tie my hands, Mrs. Hobbes. I'm asking you to trust my judgment. Tell me everything and rely on me to figure out what does matter and what I can ignore as nonsense. Believe me, it's a thing I'm good at."

Daphne softened but only to the extent that in her answer to Schmitty she spoke without anger. Her firmness stood undiminished.

"I do not doubt your acumen, Inspector," she said. "There are, however, minimal decencies. We shall talk about anything else you choose, but anything that is to be said about the money will have to wait."

"Lady, I've got a murderer on the loose. Nothing can wait. Now or later, what are we waiting for?"

"My nephew must be here. I will have no talk of it in his absence."

Schmitty turned and looked pointedly at Roderick-Pagnell's back.

"Your nephew is here," he said.

"I refer to my late husband's nephew, Gordon Hobbes. You won't have long to wait, Inspector. He should have been back by now. I can't think what's been keeping him, but it can't be much longer."

Pagnell spoke. He was only muttering and he was still keeping his back to us, but his words came through audibly enough.

"I can think, Aunt Daphne," he said. "You're just refusing to try."

"You will shut up, Roderick," Aunt Daphne ordered, "or you can leave the room."

It could have been that she was wishing there might have been some strapping nursemaid she could summon to haul an obstreperous brat off to the nursery where he could have his tantrum without annoying the adults.

Inspector Schmidt knows a stone wall when one confronts him. He doesn't batter himself bloody butting against it. He looks for a way to go around it.

"All right," he said. "That will have to wait then. It's only one possible thought. What about enemies? Do you have any enemies you know of?"

"There are those who would say that to know me is to hate me," Daphne said.

Her pleased complacency might have represented enjoyment of the thought. It was more likely that it reflected relief at the change of subject.

The inspector could hardly be satisfied with that. He needed something more specific.

"Anyone you can name?" he asked.

"Everyone has enemies, Inspector. Just as an example, there are those apes, Gillian's other tenants."

"Gibbons, his wife, Eric?"

"Yes, Gibbons and not apes. My mistake. I must be distraught. Ordinarily I am not weak in zoology. It's one of my special interests. You might even call it a hobby."

"Maybe we all of us do have enemies," Schmitty broke in, working at it. "It can be. I wouldn't say, but most people's enemies just let it go at disliking them, even hating them. They maybe eat their hearts out with it, but they don't put themselves to the expense and the risk of hiring killers. We're not talking about someone who just might have taken a dislike to you. We're talking about someone who wants you dead and who, more than that, would undertake the danger and the cost involved in hiring Jackson to put a rifle slug through you. This isn't any cheap, shoestring operation. The operating costs alone come to something, the rent on the apartment, an expensive rifle used and discarded, a row of potted plants that must have cost a mint and that were put out on the balcony just so Jackson could have a screen behind which he could watch you and not himself be seen. Add Jackson's fee. He isn't working cheap. Killers don't."

I listened to him and silently I was applauding. This was one of Inspector Schmidt's virtuoso performances. The lady refused to talk about money, so Schmitty turned to other things. Could he help it if everything led right back to money?

Daphne sighed.

"I would like to help you, Inspector," she said. "Even if you weren't telling me that my life depends on it, I should like to help you, but I'm sorry. I'm simply at a loss."

"Nobody?"

"I can think and think. Mrs. Thingumabob abominates me and she makes no secret of it. She slanders me at the bridge table, telling her bridge partners shocking lies about me. Lord Noddlewit has never forgiven me for the time I told him he was a pompous bore. I could go on and on. People who might, if they heard I'd been shot, say a chirpy 'good riddance,' I dare say you could find those by the dozens, but there isn't a one of them who would be any good to you."

"You're sure of that?" Schmitty asked.

"They don't hate me enough and they're not the sort of people who would ever do anything about it, even if they did hate me that much."

She paused, smiling at the thought of her enemies. She was a woman who relished having them. They were evidence that the barbs she had aimed at them one time or another had not fallen wide of the mark. Thinking about it, she launched one of those barbs of hers at large.

"When you speak of the expense," she said, "you rule out all of them. They're a mean lot. I can't imagine a one of them going into pocket for anything."

There was more of the same. She did us a catalog of fools she had refused to suffer, snobs she had put down, pomposities she had deflated, and rascals she had snubbed. I was beginning to wonder how long she would be able to keep it going and how long, if she didn't run down, Inspector Schmidt would go on holding still for it, but neither she nor he was put to the test.

Gordon Hobbes arrived and his arrival put a period to it. He had changed. Despite the length of time he had been away, however, it could have been nothing but a quick change. Although he had made the switch into daytime clothes, it had been a careless switch. No man in his right mind would ever have worn that tie with that shirt, and to tie a tie that badly a man would have to have been not only without a mirror but with hands that had failed to develop the necessarily opposed thumbs. A dog or a cat could have done no worse a job of it. He hadn't stopped to shave. What I was seeing was not only a contrast to the way he had been those few hours before. I was remembering the times I had seen him across the garden in jeans and a sweatshirt. He had always looked arrestingly well groomed.

He came dashing in. With time out for only a lightning dab at kissing his aunt, he zeroed in on the inspector.

"I must talk to you, Inspector," he said, and urgency boiled up through his words. "I called police headquarters and I looked for you at the house. Over there they told me you had come up here to see Daph."

"We've been waiting for you," Schmitty said.

He was talking more to Daphne than to the young man.

He was letting her know that he had agreed to wait this long but that now the time had come.

"I know," the young man apologized. "I've been tearing around and getting nowhere and then I started looking for you. I should have thought to ring Daph. I might have known she was likely to have heard from you."

The inspector turned to Daphne.

"Now, Mrs. Hobbes," he said.

Even now she was visibly reluctant to open it up. The moment she took for steeling herself to begin gave Gordon Hobbes his chance.

"Inspector," he said, "my aunt doesn't have anything she can tell you. She doesn't know. This whole thing is my fault. I should have told you last night, but stupidly I didn't. You must listen to me now."

"I'm listening," the inspector said.

X

"Before I even got to the house last night," Gordon began, "I knew what was going on. The radio report told me all I needed to know. A shot fired into Daph's drawing room through the garden window. Mrs. Armitage, wearing one of Daph's negligees, shot and killed. It had to be that she was shot by mistake. It had to be that the bullet was meant for my aunt."

Daphne interrupted him.

"Of course, Gordon, you thought it was the Gibbons lad," she said. "We all of us thought that, but the inspector has discovered otherwise."

"And meanwhile he let him get away," Pagnell added, again sending his words at us by bouncing them off the window.

"Shut up, Roderick," his aunt ordered. "We're having none of that."

"I knew it wasn't the boy," Gordon told Daphne. "You and Mrs. Armitage, the same height, very much the same figure, your white hair and the bleach job she had almost the same. I remembered that under artificial light there was no discernible difference."

"Please, Gordon," his aunt begged, "don't go on about it. I've been thinking of nothing else. Gillian would be alive today if she hadn't been mistaken for me. It's a shattering thought. A frightening thought, but that's only a part of it. It's a heartbreaking thought as well. Gillian is dead and I cannot but feel that I am to blame."

"Not you, my darling. Me."

Schmitty moved in to take control.

"Come on, man," he said. "You've got something to tell me. Get it said."

"It's my uncle's estate, Inspector, my uncle Gordon. He was Aunt Daph's husband. He made what I suppose is a peculiarly English will. You know, eldest son, primogeniture, next male in the blood line. Not that anything was entailed or anything like that, but it was the idea."

Daphne couldn't take it.

"Gordon," she said. "This is ridiculous. Being idiotic—I expect it of Roderick. From you?"

"Daph, you must let me finish. I'm not enjoying this."

"Nor am I," Daphne snapped.

It was the tone I'd heard her use on Roderick. I had a feeling that this might have been the first time Gordon Hobbes would have been taking the lash of it.

The other nephew had come away from his window and was now turned facing us. The look of fury and frustration had left him. He was now wearing a look of triumph. His not quite suppressed smirk was saying, "I told you so."

"I'm sorry," Gordon murmured. He turned back to Inspector Schmidt. "Uncle Gordon's entire estate," he explained, "was left in trust. Oh, there were bequests to servants and some other people like secretaries; and there were his personal things, links and studs, his watch, his golf clubs, some of his books, those he left directly to me. I'm talking about the residue and that is a large fortune, Inspector, even after taxes a very large fortune. All of that went into the trust. The income of it goes to his widow, my aunt, for life. On her death the trust dissolves and the principal, unencumbered, was to come to me."

"Was to?" Schmitty echoed. "Not is to?"

A fine grammatical point, nothing that could be expected to concern Inspector Schmidt. The inspector would be the last man to be fanatical about English usage. I had to think that the inspector was asking whether the young man had in mind the legal principle that says a murderer cannot inherit from his victim. Obviously it would apply to the man who hired a killer to do the murder for him.

That, however, was not what the heir had in mind. He elucidated his "was to."

"Some time ago," he said. "It's been almost four years now. I needed money, a great sum of money. It was a business opportunity, the kind of thing that doesn't come a man's way more than once in a lifetime if it comes at all, and I was in a perfect position to bring it off. All I needed was the capital. I realized the capital, Inspector, by the sale of my expectations."

"When the time comes," Schmitty asked, "the estate won't go to you? It will go to the man who bought it from you?"

Daphne gasped. I looked at her and saw what I had never expected to see. There were tears in her eyes and her lips were trembling.

"Gordon," she faltered. "You didn't. How could you?"

"I'm sorry, Daph, but I did. Looking back on it now, I ask myself why. I didn't need it. I had my job. It was a good enough job. I was making more than sufficient for my needs. My future? That was taken care of. The day would necessarily come when Uncle Gordon's money would dump down on me. I was going to be filthy rich one day and until then I could go on as I was and be more than comfortable. I was in no hurry. But I know what it was. It was vanity."

Roderick put his word in.

"Or greed," he said.

I'm sure Daphne heard him, but she let him go unrebuked. Gordon heard and thought about it for a moment.

"No, Rick," he said, sounding as though he had weighed it and had come to a carefully considered conclusion. "It was vanity. I was settling for far less. Of course, using the capital, I had every expectation of making it grow into a great deal more, but that was going to take time and even my most sanguine expectations didn't look to make it as much as I was giving up. As it worked out, it's done better than my wildest expectations, but it will still never build to the size of Uncle Gordon's estate. No, it was vanity."

Daphne took a grip on herself.

"Gordon," she said. "I don't understand. I very much want to understand."

"Yes," Gordon said. "I was afraid you wouldn't understand. I hoped you could, but, whether you could or not, I had to tell the inspector. I had this feeling and I hated it, the feeling that I was just marking time and waiting around for you to die. I don't mean I was impatient for it, quite the contrary. I suppose I was thinking that I knew how I felt and I hoped you knew how I felt, but I worried about how I looked. Did it seem to other people that I was just sitting on my expectations and doing nothing with my life?"

"I can understand that, but nevertheless . . ." Daphne said.

"I know," Gordon told her. "I felt it, something like a betrayal. I'd like to make you understand what I mean by vanity. It was an opportunity to prove myself. I saw it as a chance to be like Uncle Gordon. He made it through his own genius, through his own efforts. I wanted to do that."

"He started with inherited money," Daphne said.

"And I started with what I realized on my future inheritance. Is it so very different?"

"You didn't tell me. I would have been happy to lend you the money."

"Out of income, Daph? I needed more than you could ever have managed out of income and I needed it all at once."

"But you should have told me."

"I was afraid you'd be hurt, and, of course, you are. I was afraid you'd take it that I held Uncle Gordon and all he'd done for me cheap, even that I saw him only as a source of money and that his warmth and his affection meant nothing to me."

"How else can I take it?"

She was asking him to tell her, to find a way for her so that she could look at it and it would be less painful to her.

"It's not that unprecedented," he said. "It's done all the time. Back home there's an established company that does it as a regular business, investing in reversions, more than one such company in fact. I've heard of one that's called Bird in Hand. I should have taken a quick trip over and gone to them. It would have been all right then."

"I can see no difference," Daph murmured.

"Where I went wrong is I found someone over here. An established firm that has this sort of thing as its only business has its funds revolving all the time, money paid out to people like me, estates coming in. One deal might liquidate quickly. Another might take longer than the average. All of that is contained in their calculations. They wouldn't get impatient. They'd work on an actuarial basis."

Daphne got to her feet and stumbled toward one of the suite's bedrooms. From the little I could see of it when she opened the door it was obviously a bedroom. Gordon started to follow her, but the inspector held him back. She went through into the room and shut the door behind her.

"You can talk to your aunt later," Schmitty said. "I need to keep her alive so you can talk to her. I'm waiting for a name. I should have had it last night."

"I know, Inspector, I know," Gordon groaned. "I've been all mixed up in my thinking. I'm still getting my priorities straight."

"Leave your priorities for later. Who did you sell to?"

"A man named Johnson."

That triggered me. "Johnson?" I said. "Or was it Jackson?"

"Johnson."

"And he hired a hit man with a sense of humor," Schmitty said. "Taking on an alias for the job, the hit man had his own little private joke, calling himself Jack Jackson." He turned back to Gordon Hobbes. "You know where I can find this Johnson?" he asked.

"He's left the country. That's where I've been, looking for him."

"Where did you look?"

"His office. It's down on East Forty-first Street."

He gave the address.

"That Johnson," Schmitty said. "You know how to pick them. What did you think you could do if you found him? Tell him to behave himself?"

"You know him?" Gordon asked.

"Big business," Schmitty answered, "and he's no damn good at it. Just when he's riding high, he gets himself overextended or something, but when anyone else would go bust, your Johnson never does. There's a bank robbery or a big jewelry job in one of the best hotels and he isn't in trouble anymore. Everything has always led to him and nothing's ever been pinned on him, but this time he's mine and with more to go on than the robbery people ever had. You'll testify?"

"Of course I'll testify, but what good? He's skipped the country."

"He'll be back or we'll bring him back. That can be handled. There's still my question. What did you think you were doing when you went looking for him?"

"Buy him out. What he gave me plus heavy interest for the time since. Anything. As much as he wanted to call the deal off. It seemed to me that the first priority had to be eliminating the danger to Daph."

"When he's hurting for money and hurting so much that

he goes to murder, anything would have to be one hell of a lot," Schmitty remarked.

"I told you I've done well. If necessary, I could liquidate everything. I can do it and no regrets. I don't need it. I've had what I wanted. I proved to myself I could make it."

"And Mrs. Armitage?" Schmitty asked. "Just the luck of the game?"

"I was wrong. I know I was wrong. I just couldn't think of anything but Aunt Daph. I had to be sure she was safe. I figured Mrs. Armitage would be my leverage. I could offer him a lot of money but never as much as he would have by waiting. Maybe since he didn't want to wait, it would have been enough. I expected it wouldn't be, but with the alternative that I would tell you, I thought he'd take the money and run."

"And that would square everything?"

"Of course it wouldn't, but I was counting on the police, on you, to catch up with it. Until you did, I'd have had Daph out of danger."

"We were going to do it with no help from you?"

"I don't know that I thought that far ahead. I suppose I was too frightened for Daph to think properly. I suppose that was going to depend on how well you did. If I saw that you needed what I could tell you, I was going to tell you."

"Regardless of the deal you would have made with Johnson?"

"I was going to make the best ideal with him I could, but except for paying him the money, I was never going to feel that the deal was binding on me. The bloke got a woman killed. He tried to kill Daph. Nothing I could ever do would be playing him too dirty."

"I hope you'll remember that when testifying time comes."

"I'll remember it. It's something I'm not likely to forget,

not ever. Anyhow, I made no deal with him. I couldn't find him. So there's no question there."

"You say he's left the country. Is that what they told you at his office?"

"They said he was out of the country. They didn't know when he would be back. They didn't know where he was or where he could be reached. He gets in touch with them. They don't get in touch with him. They explained it's the way he does when he needs a complete rest. He goes away like that and sets it up so nobody can get at him."

"Understandable," Schmitty said. "Nobody ever called me restful. Did they say when he left?"

Hobbes groaned.

"It matches up, Inspector. I've been matching the dates in my head and they're driving me out of my mind. You know about the dead-hawk business and Aunt Daph's party and the newspaper gossip piece? Three days after that piece was published."

Schmitty nodded.

"Three days for hiring his hit man and to get things set up for going away. Out of sight and out of touch until the job's been done and Eric Gibbons is arrested for a foolish murder. Then he comes back and collects."

"Exactly, Inspector," Hobbes said. "Unless they were lying to me about when he left, it had to mean he doesn't do his own killing. So he has a man here who handles it for him, and the man is out there somewhere waiting for his next chance at it so he can earn his pay and I have no way of reaching Johnson to get it stopped."

"Which left you with nothing but your last resort," Schmitty said, "coming to me."

"I make no excuses for myself. From beginning to end on this I make no excuses for myself."

Inspector Schmidt was in no mood for being sorry for the

man. Hobbes had taken too long before he'd gotten around to talking.

"Don't cry, Mr. Hobbes," he said. "You're the one who's going to do real well out of this whole mess. No court in the world will call your sale to Johnson valid. He's washed that out with murder. It's got Mrs. Armitage's blood all over it. You're sitting pretty, Mr. Hobbes. The money you got from Johnson, the money you've been making on that money, and one of these days your uncle's estate, and all it's costing you is one dead woman who wasn't even an in-law."

Gordon Hobbes winced.

"I know I'm going to have to think about that," he said, "guilt and pain and shame. It's there, but for now I'm holding it off. Now somewhere out there there's a killer and I have no way of stopping him."

The inspector went no further with rubbing it in, but Roderick Pagnell did it for him.

"It's your fault he's out there," he said. "Of course, the police were stupid, but they're always stupid. If you'd said anything about this last night while the man was still there, even the police would have been bright enough to ask who was new over there. Then he couldn't have gotten away."

Hobbes looked to the inspector. Schmitty let it stand. Swallowing hard, Hobbes found his voice.

"All right if I go in and talk to Daph?" he asked.

"If you want to," the inspector said.

Hobbes went to the bedroom door and knocked. There was no answer. He knocked again, and again there was nothing. He turned away from the door.

"I'll wait till she wants to talk to me," he said, "if ever."

The inspector had other ideas. He went to the door and shouldered Hobbes away from it. Schmitty didn't knock. He pounded. He would have needed to put only a little more force into it to have beaten the door down.

"Don't, Inspector," Hobbes protested. "If she wants to be alone . . ."

Schmitty ignored the protest. He pounded again and this time he shouted.

"Mrs. Hobbes. You don't have to come out if you don't want to and we won't come in. I just have to know if you're all right."

No response. Inspector Schmidt could just go on having to know.

"Mrs. Hobbes," he tried again. "All you have to do is tell me. Say you're all right and we won't disturb you. Unless you say something, I'm coming in."

Hobbes was outraged.

"Inspector, you can't," he said.

"Damn well right I can," Schmitty told him.

He turned the knob and flung the door open. The bedroom was empty. Directly across it was a bathroom. The bathroom door was standing ajar and the bathroom, too, was empty.

The inspector went storming into the bedroom with me at his heels. Hobbes hung back. I heard him muttering something about privacy, but Pagnell brushed past Hobbes and came in behind me. Inspector Schmidt's survey of the room took no more than a moment. Immediately he had spotted the door he wanted. He dove at it and wrenched it open. It opened on a hotel corridor and directly across the corridor was a swinging door and a sign on it that said STAIRS.

The corridor was empty. There was nobody in sight. There wasn't much of it, only the short leg of the L it formed with the main corridor. The inspector stamped out that way. He had forgotten that he was without his shoes. Pounding socked feet against heavy hotel carpeting doesn't give a man anything you could call satisfying stamping.

The police officer was still at his station outside the suite's main door. He hadn't seen Mrs. Hobbes. He'd seen no one since we'd arrived but Mr. Hobbes, her nephew, the one who brought her to the hotel. Mr. Hobbes had come in. Nobody had gone out.

"The other door," the inspector stormed. "Hasn't anybody been on the other door?"

The cop blinked.

"What other door, sir?" he asked. "There ain't any other door, Inspector."

"Around the corner." Schmitty was roaring at the man. "Nobody had the sense to look around the corner."

The door at the cop's back opened and Gordon Hobbes came out. He had heard Schmitty's roaring. He couldn't have missed. The way doors were opening and shutting all up and down the corridor, it was a good bet that the hotel desk was about to be flooded with complaints.

"There was no need to do anything about the bedroom doors, Inspector," Hobbes said, coming to the support of the poor embattled cop. "They are solid metal doors, bolted shut. Nobody could get in through those without breaking them down and that would be a noise to rouse the whole hotel before you could put more than a dent in them."

"The one in her bedroom isn't bolted now," Schmitty said, brushing past Hobbes.

He had to go in to retrieve his shoes.

"She was to be protected against someone coming in on her," Hobbes persisted. "Nobody could have thought that we needed to make a prisoner of her for her own protection."

"I know. I know. But now we better find her, and quick," Schmitty said.

"The man?" Hobbes asked, trying to talk himself away from fear. "He can't possibly know she was here."

"Let's not count on it," Schmitty said. "Everything's telling me he does know."

He was back out in the corridor, hitting elevator call buttons. A car came up and the four of us piled into it. There was a time when there would have been an operator to question, but that was before progress had depopulated hotel elevators. There was nothing but pushbuttons and they could give no answers.

"How?" Hobbes asked while we were riding down to the lobby. "How could he possibly know?"

The inspector turned to Pagnell.

"The last anyone saw of the man," he said, "was when you were there making your big noise about your blood-kin right to know where your aunt had been taken. You found out and you took off up here. Did you watch to see if you were being followed?"

Pagnell blustered.

"Why would I watch?" he said. "The one man in the world who had the most to gain from her death, you let him take her away from you. I was concerned for her safety, not for doing your work for you."

The inspector turned to me.

"A woman needs nephews," he said. "I don't know what we would have done without their help."

Gordon Hobbes said nothing. He was just going white around the lips and breaking out in a sweat. Roderick Pagnell also had nothing further to say. He had distributed his needles. He could savor in silence the way they had gone in.

By the elevator bank in the lobby there was the usual starter, a fine figure of a man in a uniform General Patton might have coveted. I'd often wondered what these starters were good for. This one proved to be of some use.

He hadn't seen Mrs. Hobbes. Yes, he would know her if he saw her. His relief had called in sick and he was working a double shift. He had been on duty when she arrived during the night and, with all the instructions there had been about letting nobody up to the twenty-third floor without an okay from the desk, he had taken special notice of the lady.

If she had come down in any of the elevators, he would most certainly have seen her. Sunday wasn't the busiest day of the week and this wasn't the busiest hour of the day. For an hour and more, traffic on the elevators had been light. He had seen everyone who came out of them.

"The fire stairs alongside room twenty-three seventeen?" the inspector asked. "Where do they let out?"

"Around the corner," the flunky answered. "You'll see an alleyway. In there."

"If Mrs. Hobbes comes down in one of the elevators or any way she comes," Schmitty ordered, "hold her here till I come back. Even if you have to knock her down and sit on her, don't let her get away from you."

The man's jaw dropped and he sputtered and stammered. Inspector Schmidt had no time for that. The nephews had already taken off but the inspector wasn't likely to think that they would be sufficient. We raced across the lobby and out to the street. Hobbes and Pagnell, running neck and neck, were just turning the corner. We took off after them.

When we came around the corner they were just hitting the alley. It was only a couple of hundred feet down the block, but it seemed to me that we were forever getting there. It wasn't that we weren't running hard. It felt as though we might have been making Olympic time for the distance, but you know how it is when you are under strain. Each second can seem an eternity.

We reached the head of the alley and everything happened at once. Daphne Hobbes was at the fire exit, but it looked to me as though she wasn't coming out. She was on her way back in and she was running. Jackson was down the alley, not ten feet away from her and closing in fast, but Gordon Hobbes was in there too, and he was faster. He was almost near enough to reach out and grapple with Jackson.

Pagnell was not far behind them and he had a gun in his hand. Schmitty thundered past him. Just after the inspector had gone by, Pagnell raised his gun and fired and it was crazy. He didn't have the muzzle pointed at Jackson. He had taken a bead on Gordon Hobbes instead.

The smallest split of a second later, Jackson fired. Schmitty had his gun out and was closing in on Jackson and Hobbes. I saw Pagnell taking aim for a second shot.

I dove for him. Things were getting too congested down the alley and I could just see the slob hitting someone this time with the odds all too good that it wouldn't be Jackson. I was just too late. He got his shot off and this time there could be no doubt about it. It wasn't that in incompetence in gun handling he was anything like my equal. I could see where he was aiming and he was dead on. He was trying for the easiest target, his man's trunk, and the man he was trying for was Gordon Hobbes.

I grappled with him and tore the gun away from him. Somewhere in there—as I remember it, it was just before I got my hands on Pagnell—Jackson squeezed off a second shot, but that one went into the air. Even as Hobbes was taken down by Pagnell's bullet, Schmitty had vaulted over the fallen man's body and had hit Jackson's arm. That was the only reason why Jackson's second shot went high and was again a miss.

I was tied up holding Pagnell and the inspector was wrestling Jackson to the ground. So it was Daphne who ran to Gordon where he lay on the alley pavement. I was certain he was on the way out if he wasn't already gone. I had that clear picture of where Pagnell had aimed.

All those shots, of course, brought people running. Cops, hotel staff, passersby, they flooded in on us. I turned Pagnell over to one of the officers.

"Hold him," I said. "Inspector Schmidt will want the louse."

Pagnell tried to shake free.

"I'm not going anywhere," he said.

"Damn right you aren't. I'll testify and it's murder."

"For shooting at Jackson? The man's a killer. He would have murdered my aunt."

I didn't stop to tell him it was a good story but that it was going to come up against me. I was the eyewitness who would stop any chance of his making it stick. At that moment I was more interested in Gordon Hobbes.

I ran down the alley. A couple of officers had taken Jackson off the inspector's hands and Schmitty was now with Daphne Hobbes kneeling beside Gordon, bending over him. Gordon was alive. He was even talking.

"I'm all right," he was saying. "What about you, Daph? I saw that he missed with his first shot. Handguns aren't as reliable as rifles and he was hurrying it. But he did get off a second shot. I was diving for his legs. No time for anything but trying to knock him off his feet before he could shoot. I was diving for his legs, but I know I didn't make it. Something knocked me on my bum. I suppose it was this."

He indicated the ooze of blood that was soaking the shoulder of his jacket.

I knew how to clear away his confusion.

"Pagnell," I said. "He was shooting to kill and he was aiming dead on you. It was diving for Jackson that saved you. If you'd been going after him standing up, you would have taken the slug in your chest or your belly. I thought you had. I was sure you were gone."

Schmitty glanced up the alley where Pagnell was being pompously indignant. At my back I could hear Jackson. He was still working on the Mr. Law-and-order image. He was protesting that he had been there only for the protection of Daphne Hobbes. He was pushing the thought that he had come along to the hotel to see if he could help and that, on looking it over, he had seen that the front of the building was well protected but the alley was uncovered. He hadn't been shooting at Daphne. He had seen her come running out of the fire exit and, thinking that she was being pursued, he had been firing in an effort to stop her pursuers.

The inspector ignored both of the professed innocents. It was too obvious that neither of their stories would ever stand up. He spoke to Gordon Hobbes instead.

"It doesn't look bad," he said. "No arterial bleeding and it looks like it didn't hit bone."

Gordon moved to sit up, but Daphne wasn't having any of that. She pushed him back.

"Lie still you fool," she said. "I can't do without you."

"That's right," Schmitty added. "I can't do without you either. I'll need your testimony. We'll have an ambulance here in a minute." He turned to Daphne. "Speaking of fools," he said, "what did you think you were up to sneaking out of the hotel?"

"I needed to be alone. I needed to think."

"Bedroom wasn't alone enough?"

"I was suffocating in there. I had to get out."

"Even when I'd told you Jackson was on the loose and still gunning for you?"

"It never occurred to me that he could know to come here. How did he know?"

"He followed your nephew Roderick. I don't know how he could have known you'd come out this way. We'll have to work on that."

"But he didn't," Daphne said. "I came out and walked through to the street. I saw him at the corner of the road. He was there, watching both ways, the hotel entrance and down here. He saw me and started for me. I ran back in here."

Schmitty grinned.

"Then we don't have to work on it," he said, "and I'm glad I don't have to keep track of you anymore, lady. You had me fooled. Okay, out the bedroom door and not around to the elevators because the man we had on your door out there

would see you. The way I had it figured, it would be down
one flight by the fire stairs and the elevator the rest of the
way. Nobody walks down twenty-three flights of stairs."

Daphne grinned back at him.

"I do, Inspector dear," she said. "In the first place, it's
only twenty-two flights. The silly dolts have no thirteenth
floor. You must understand. I'm English, after all. I'm not all
that addicted to lifts. Walking is English. I always go walking when I need to think."

"You were in a spot where you should have left the thinking to the inspector," I said.

"You came close to getting two people killed," Schmitty
added, "yourself and this nephew of yours."

"I know," she said. "That idiot Roderick."

"More an opportunist than an idiot," I said. "He was
going to let Jackson kill you while he shot away at Gordon.
The timing was tricky, but he came close to making it. His
idea was that he could kill Gordon just in the split second
before Jackson got his shot off at you. Then he'd have it
made every which way. Not his fault that he wasn't as good
as he should be at moving targets."

"He would have had the perfect story," Schmitty agreed.
"It would have been that he was trying to save you by getting Jackson. Hobbes got in the way and caught the bullet
and that was too bad. Pagnell would be no end sorry about
Hobbes' death but he would also make it clear that if
Hobbes had stayed out of the way, his bullet would have
brought Jackson down before Jackson could have gotten
you."

"I see," Daphne said. "Gordon would have been dead before me and everything would have gone to Roderick, my
only surviving relative."

"And if he could have managed it," Schmitty said,
finishing it for her, "he would also have killed Jackson and
made himself a hero."

"Yes," Gordon said. "It would be that he had done his best and it was only my clumsiness that spoiled things. I got in the way and took the shot meant for Jackson and that disposed of me, but Jackson had the time to kill you, and, because of me, he couldn't get to Jackson in time, but he did his best. Better late than never and all that. Not half clever, our Roderick."

Daphne shook her head.

"You're confusing me," she said. "You mean your estate man didn't? Was it Roderick who hired Jackson?"

"No," Schmitty said. "Back there Roderick was doing nothing."

"Just eating his heart out because there would be all that money going to Gordon and not to him," I suggested.

"But only that," Schmitty continued. "Then he heard about Mrs. Armitage and he got the idea that if it was Gordon trying to get you killed or even if he could somehow convince the law that it was Gordon, that might break your husband's trust and the money would come to him."

"I see," Daphne murmured. She turned to me. "That's what you meant, George, my sweet, when you called him an opportunist. Upstairs he learned that it was no good. There wasn't a chance he could fit Gordon to a frame. That's the way you say it, isn't it? 'Fit Gordon to a frame?' Then down here he saw his chance. First Gordon dead and then I'm dead and he's the heir and not even any waiting time." She sighed. "I'm glad it's over. It's been most unpleasant."

The ambulance had come and Gordon was being moved to a stretcher.

"Not over," he said. "There's still Johnson."

"You can forget him," Schmitty said, "but only until you're called to testify. I'll get Johnson, whether it'll be when he comes back or on extradition. Jackson will talk and you'll testify. Johnson's out of business this time."

Daphne walked along beside the stretcher as they carried Gordon to the ambulance. She was holding his hand.

"There's also Gillian," she said. "She was a strumpet, but I was fond of her. I shall miss her."

She said nothing about what I knew she was thinking, that she would be haunted by the feeling that was almost guilt since it was because of her that Jill Armitage had died. Whatever such feelings she would have, she was recognizing that like feelings would be eating at Gordon Hobbes.

Daphne could be tactful when she chose to be.